## TARGET ZONE

Mack Bolan checked out the terminal area. He punched the Fire Enable control on the command console and waited for the green light. The sequence was perfect—Fire Enable Go—Target Acquisition Positive . . . the rocket launchers were ready.

And, he had his targets—Mafia men on the flight deck of the airport. The first rocket rustled away, a flaming arrow streaking unerringly along the target path in an awesome rush of doom! The men had but a brief, flashing impression of some object streaking across the area before the explosion.

"It's an ambush! We've got fire behind us! That's our cars burning back there!" one man screamed, reaching for his gun. But he needn't have bothered. The second rocket ripped into the fuel truck. Men were thrown from the impact, and lay blistering from the flames.

Above the continuous muzzle blasts and explosions, a conversation could be heard.

"Mack Bolan is back."

"Back where?"

"Back where he started."

Could anyone doubt it?

## The Executioner Series:

# the
# EXECUTIONER
# #28

## SAVAGE FIRE
### by Don Pendleton

PINNACLE BOOKS       NEW YORK CITY

EXECUTIONER #28: SAVAGE FIRE

*Copyright © 1977 by Pinnacle Books, Inc.*

All rights reserved, including the right to reproduce this book or portions thereof in any form.

An original Pinnacle Books edition, published for the first time anywhere.

ISBN: 0-523-40-016-5

First printing, March 1977

Cover illustration by Gil Cohen

*Printed in the United States of America*

PINNACLE BOOKS, INC.
275 Madison Avenue
New York, N.Y. 10016

*Dedication:*

For my son, Derek,
on the occasion of his 13th birthday.
The fire, my son,
awaits every young man.
Be there.

              dp

The civilized man is a more
experienced and wiser savage.
    —Henry David Thoreau

Has any man ever attained to
inner harmony by pondering the
experience of others? Not since
the world began! He must pass
through the fire.
    —Norman Douglas

Savages do not move themselves
to the fire. I will bring the
fire to them. Then we shall see
whether they grow or burn.
    —Mack Bolan, the Executioner

# TABLE OF CONTENTS

# SAVAGE FIRE

# PROLOGUE

The big man stood in darkness and stared at darkness while thinking of home.

The night was wet and the small cemetery, bathed in a driving rain, seemed set in a world apart.

It was.

The single headstone marking the family plot spoke to another time and another place; it spoke of home and all that word had once implied to the tall, still man in the dripping poncho. It spoke, yes, of pride and simple dignity, love and human warmth—care and sympathy and understanding. It spoke of home, yes, but the word was now no more than the dying echo of an irretrievable past; worst, it was an almost unbearable taunt at the horizon of a hopeless future.

A world apart, sure.

Mack Bolan had lived wholly in the *Now* for an eternity, it seemed. There was no Now in this burial ground; there were but the Past and the Future. Both were present here, patiently awaiting the homecoming of the warrior.

Yeah. There lay Mack Bolan's home.

Perfectly fitting, too, it seemed. He had consciously chosen the course which had brought him inevitably deeper into this melancholy realm of the dead. Knowingly and deliberately, he had renounced the light for the darkness.

Why?

He did not know why. He knew only that he had responded to his understanding of duty. Duty. Such an ambiguous word. Was it a man's duty to damn himself to the dark and savage Now? And how much damnation could the human soul endure? Mack Bolan was more than *thrice* damned. The man was a walking damnation—or such was his understanding. How many hundreds of graves such as this had he filled with the results of his *duty* in the *Now*? Thousands, probably. Long ago he had passed beyond feeling that there was any meaning to the count. It was a war of attrition, sure. One did not count the dead in such a war. One counted only the living—and Bolan had ceased even that meaningless endeavor. The living enemy was infinite; there was no meaning to their numbers.

Could there, then, be a meaning to his war?

Perhaps. Perhaps.

The chiseled, expressionless face moved suddenly in recognition of an altered quality of the night. The utter blackness was relieved only now and then by occasional flashes of distant lightning. The rain was heavy and all pervasive, producing the only sounds of this stygian moment. But the big guy had become aware of another presence in the Now. He moved almost imperceptibly, bringing the black snout of the Beretta Belle to a slit in the poncho as a stealthy figure materialized in the wet atmosphere.

A quiet voice which remained one of the few living echoes of the past announced, "It's me, Sarge."

Meaning, yeah—there was meaning enough.

2

Bolan's taut figure relaxed as the two stood toe to toe in the downpour, smiling grimly at each other through the universal solvent.

"I was getting worried about you, Leo," the big man said—the voice at once warm and cold, glad and sad.

"Sorry. I had to break a trail." The underboss of western Massachusetts grimaced as he added, "The jungle is closing fast."

"I noticed," Bolan agreed. "Who is it?"

"It's Augie, I think."

Bolan pursed his lips for a faint whistle. "That bad, eh?"

"In spades, yeah. It's going down big, everywhere. Not just here. I just happened to get caught in the ringer. There's no figuring the safe zones, Sarge."

"There are none," Bolan replied grimly, adding, ". . . in this world." He sighed. "So what are you reading, Leo?"

The little guy spread his hands in a gesture of hopelessness. "End of the trail," he muttered. "I guess Hal was right. There's no game without a sponsor. The game is over."

"Get a new sponsor," Bolan quietly suggested.

The Mafia chieftain shook his head. "Against Augie? No way. Not in this part of the world. That's the entire idea behind the purge. Naw. It's over. Anyway, thanks for coming." His eyes swept the burial plot. "Sorry to bring you back to all this pain for nothing. It's a hell of a homecoming, isn't it. You'd better get out while you can, buddy. This whole territory will be closed by daybreak."

"What will you do, Leo?"

"Play Hal's game, I guess. Damned shame. I was

3

expecting an installation on *La Commissione* within another few months. But . . ."

Bolan asked, "What is Hal's game?"

"Hal" was Harold Brognola, an upper echelon official in the U.S. Department of Justice—Leo Turrin's secret boss.

"I'll come out of the closet," the undercover cop explained. "It's too soon, sure—but it's the only game left."

Bolan shook his head. "Won't work, Leo. Soon as Augie discovers you're a talking head, he'll collect it. He'll have your make the instant you step out of the closet. You know that and Hal knows that."

The little guy tried to smile, and almost made it. "He'll have to find it first, won't he."

"Don't talk like a junior G-man," Bolan quietly scolded him. "That old man will call in every tab in the country. He'll have senators and congressmen doubling as hitmen if that's what it takes. Hal doesn't even know which of his own people he can trust. You don't seriously believe that Augie Marinello is going to sit serenely and watch his empire get dismantled brick by brick in a courtroom."

"That's the hell of it," Turrin groused. "We aren't even sure we can do it. And it could take ten years of legal maneuvering. By that time . . ."

"You won't be in the game for ten minutes," Bolan assured him.

Turrin's face mirrored the truth of those words as he replied, "It's the only game we have, Sarge. We'll just have to risk it."

"It isn't a matter of risk," Bolan argued. "It's a dead certainty."

"Sure, sure," the undercover fed muttered, tiring of the argument.

"Where's Angelina and the kids?"

4

"They're covered."

"Only while you are," Bolan pointed out.

"They're safed," Turrin growled.

"Nothing is safed. You know that better than anybody."

"I—I don't know, Sarge. I just don't know. What the hell else can I—?"

"Dig a hole in that closet, Leo. I'll find you another sponsor."

The guy chuckled nervously. "I respect you more than any man I've ever known, Sarge. But, well, there are limits to everything. It's too much. And it's time to call the game—*my* game, not yours. What's the profit if we both go down on this count?"

That sense of "respect" worked both ways. Leo Turrin was among the toughest and the most courageous men in Bolan's experience—and there had been many as models for comparison. It was, sure, a hard game—a hell of a hard game, from any point of view. The guy had been poised at the edge of a knife for years, playing the double game in the largest league there was. Maybe he was tiring, though. Maybe he was actually glad that the game was ending.

"What do you *want*, Leo? Would you like to save the game?"

"Sure I would. What kind of question is that?"

"Okay," Bolan said tiredly. "You owe me, buddy."

"Granted. I owe you plenty. That's why I say—"

"I want your life, Leo. Not your death."

The two solemnly regarded each other through a long silence broken only by the distant rumbling of the heavens and the unbroken tattoo of falling raindrops. Presently, Turrin chuckled and broke

5

contact with those glowing eyes. "Okay," he said lightly. "Okay."

"How much longer can you hold out?"

The little guy shrugged and pulled his raincoat tighter. "I told you. Daybreak, if I'm lucky."

"Let's talk again at daybreak, then."

"Don't, uh, try anything crazy. Not on my account, friend."

"Don't start talking sanity to me, Leo."

Turrin laughed again. A lightning flash briefly illumined the grave marker at his friend's side, the name BOLAN seemingly wreathed in a halo of fire for that electric instant. "You're right," he muttered. "It's too late, now, for sanity. Okay. What do you have in mind?"

Bolan shrugged and displayed a grim smile. "I'll try to buy you some more time in that closet, *mafioso*. We'll play the ear from there."

Turrin smiled back as he tiredly commented, "You just don't know how to say quit, do you. Okay. Daybreak it is. Standard routine?"

Bolan nodded. "Hit my floater at five past every hour until we connect."

Turrin reached out with both hands. Bolan gripped them tightly. "Stay hard, Leo," he said gruffly.

"Way to go, man," the undercover cop replied. He broke the hand grip and faded into the rainy night.

Bolan leaned against the family headstone and watched the blackness devour that lone vestige of the past.

A true friend.

Yeah, and Bolan had once been sworn to the death of that friend. Talk about *sanity*! And, no, in

6

the present circumstances, Mack Bolan did not know how to say quit.

It was a lousy homecoming, sure. But quite in keeping with the realities of the place. It had begun here. It would, inevitably, end here. But not with Bolan's willing cooperation.

"Wait a while longer," he said quietly to the grave.

In his own way, it was a sort of prayer. The closest, perhaps, that this man could come to prayer. Mack Samuel Bolan, whose name was already carved into that headstone, was not yet quite ready to return home. There remained a very important job to be done, in the eternal Now—which, in the personal understanding of the man, was simply another name for Hell.

In effect, Mack Bolan was already home.

The man who prowled the territories of hell was himself but an echo of the past.

The man who challenged hell was *the Executioner*. And, no, he did not know how to say quit.

Oh yeah, oh yeah. There was meaning to this war.

# CHAPTER ONE

## Bolan's Game

Numbers, yes—the numbers had meaning again as the big man in executioner black, practically invisible in the rainy night, made the quiet reconnaissance into no-man's-land. The time was a few minutes past ten o'clock. Here and there, throughout that suburban neighborhood, muffled light showed behind draped windows, but there was very little stirring about—an occasional automobile venturing cautiously along the rainswept streets, a dog barking nervously in the distance, now and then a light appearing at an upstairs window as the residents prepared for bed.

There was more, though, than that.

There was a vehicle with two solemn men inside parked inconspicuously at the curb a few hundred feet north of the Turrin home, another at the first intersection to the south.

They were not cops, and they were not locals.

Bolan knew who they were. They were the hounds of hell, staked out along the game trails, patiently awaiting the appearance of prey. Both cars were radio equipped. Both were lightly manned. And, yeah, Bolan had their numbers.

He quietly withdrew, returning to his own vehicle which had been discreetly stashed well clear of the stakeout zone, and drove back along the game trail—making his approach from the south in a sedate run which carried him past the stakeout vehicle there and on along the street to Leo Turrin's deserted residence.

He pulled into the drive and killed the lights, then stepped outside and moved quickly to the rear entrance. It had to look natural, of course—unsuspecting. He found the key where he knew it would be and let himself in, turning on a single light downstairs and moving immediately to the second floor where he also illuminated the master bedroom and bath. He wasted not a single motion or moment, moving quickly downstairs and through the rear to the outside, blending into the wet night for a quick quit of that place.

The hounds would already have performed their function.

Very soon, the headhunters would be on the scene.

And, sure, it was a game for which Mack Bolan had written the rulebook.

The Executioner, also, would be there. He circled on foot to the south intersection and approached the stakeout vehicle from the rear. He opened the back door and slid onto the seat, the silent Beretta leading the way. Two startled faces turned to the quiet intrusion and each immediately received a Parabellum boneshredder from the sighing Belle, dead center between flaring eyes.

Bolan reached over the seat and started the engine, turned on the parking lights, then left them there and completed the circle on foot. He scratched the other pair of hounds with the same quiet dispatch, retreating immediately to the darkness opposite the Turrin residence and settling into a patient vigil.

The wait was not long. Less than ten minutes after the lights had first appeared at Leo Turrin's windows, a big crew wagon eased in from the north—a Cadillac limousine with jumpseats, and crammed with personnel. It paused momentarily beside the stakeout car, then went on without lights to halt just short of the Turrin drive.

The vision was terrible in the constant downpour from the black skies, and even sounds were muffled and uncertain in the background of steady raindrops, but Bolan was aware of an energetic exodus from that big crew wagon as the head party descended upon its target. He caught a glimpse of two figures moving swiftly through the dim glow of light at the side of the house—then two more, close behind. The driver remained with the car—and that put four guns at the rear of the house, four at the front.

It came, then—two guys charging the front door with sawed-off shotguns at chest level, a quick kick at the door—and they were inside, briefly visible and identifiable in the sudden light before disappearing into the interior.

Real professionals, yeah—these guys knew what they were doing.

The other two remained at the front lawn—shadows, mostly, raised shotguns silhouetted against the light from the upstairs windows—waiting coolly for something to show at one of those windows.

Bolan waited, also, respectful of that professionalism, and thankful that Leo Turrin was nowhere near.

Again, the wait was not long. He moved closer as four gunners moved through that doorway and down the stairs to the lawn. Others drifted into

11

that little knot at the front of the house. Bolan was close enough now to overhear the angered words of that conference.

"Nothing's in there, Mario."

"Nothing came out the back way," reported another.

"What the hell is this?"

"Run ask Shorty Joe what the hell this is, Eddy."

One of the glistening shadows detached itself from the group at the steps and ran up the street to the stakeout car.

Bolan saw the interior light flash on as the guy jerked the door open—then the door was hurriedly slammed shut and the guy came loping back.

From ten yards out, he gaspingly reported, "They got their damn heads blowed off, Mario!"

A thick voice from the knot immediately snapped, *"Move 'em!"*

The knot abruptly dissolved and flowed toward the street. Two figures moved quickly on to the death car while the others hastily piled into the crew wagon. Engines revved, lights flashed, and both vehicles sped away.

Bolan went to his car in the Turrin driveway and moved out behind them, his own headlamps extinguished. The procession paused briefly at the first intersection as the head party made its second grim discovery. That vehicle quickly joined the lineup. Bolan fell back, giving them plenty of running room. For now, all he wanted was tracks—a game trail of his own. And, yes, the numbers suddenly had meaning again—in a tactical sense—and the Executioner was taking their count.

"Twenty headhunters," was the word in town. "Ten from Boston, ten from Albany. The meanest around."

Lucky, yes, for Leo Turrin that his ears were perceptive and his instincts active. Otherwise he and his entire family would be so much slaughtered meat at this moment, scattered in bloody little chunks about that house back there.

And, as Mack Bolan tracked that head party toward the rest of its numbers, his mind sought a logic to the lunacy.

Why, for God's sake, Pittsfield? Why here?

Léo Turrin's little Pittsfield arm could not field twenty hard men even if all had remained to fight. It was a nickel-and-dime mob, Turrin's was—pimps and bookies, policy men and juice merchants, grease and graft crews—hardly a dozen hard men among them. Pittsfield's only claim to fame—in mob circles—was Turrin himself. Bolan had broken the rest of it beyond repair, in the battle that had opened this eternal war—oh hell, how many eternities ago!—the battle that had smashed the Sergio Frenchi empire and left western Massachusetts an open territory.

Turrin had been the sole ranking survivor of that initial battle of Mack Bolan's war against the Mafia. The savage old men in new York had then looked at the territory, dismissed it, written it off as a viable property, and suffered Leo Turrin's self-elevation to underboss status in the town nobody wanted.

An underboss was not a boss. Only *La Commissione* could make a boss, and that regal council had not yet seen fit to recognize the territorial claims of Leo Turrin. Pittsfield had thus functioned as a colonial arm of the national empire, without representation at the council tables, answerable to the whims and politics of the bunch in New York.

Turrin himself, however, had grown steadily in

13

terms of national prominence and prestige—thanks mostly to his status as a "Bolan expert." Good things had lately been brewing for the guy. Augie Marinello himself, *de facto* boss of all the bosses, had taken a shine to the brash "kid" from Pittsfield and had apparently been grooming him for some exalted position in the international structure.

So what had gone sour? Why had the tables suddenly been turned? Why the big purge? And why was Leo Turrin coming down on the wrong side of the cut? It was not a personal vendetta—Bolan was sure of that. This "purge" was of a more or less national scope. The movements were being felt everywhere, not just here in Pittsfield. What the hell was happening?

It did not have to make sense. Bolan realized that. Not in this savage world of Mafia. Here, "sense" was usually only what the bosses wanted.

Right now, it seemed, what they wanted was Leo Turrin's head—and they had dispatched twenty hard men to collect it. That act in itself seemed to be saying something about the total question. The numbers did not compute. This was not the usual way. It was too many guns for what should have been a routine hit. Someone evidently felt a strong need to get to Leo Turrin hard and quick. Who? Why?

Those were secondary questions, of course. At the moment, it was purely a game of numbers. Four were down. Nine more were in the gunsights. Another seven needed to be accounted for.

Then, the universe willing, Pittsfield would send back twenty soft men.

Maybe, then, the old savages would send her forty more—and Pittsfield would need to soften and return those numbers also.

Would *eighty* then follow?

Bolan shook the question away. It needed to go to the end of the line—behind *who* and *why*.

At the moment, right now, Mack Bolan was playing the only game he had. It was one which he knew and understood, perhaps better than any other man alive.

It was, yeah, the death game.

# CHAPTER TWO

## Body Count

They were quartered at a rundown old motel just off the Berkshire Trail, east of the city—a dozen or so small cabins scattered at the edge of a wood.

The head party seemed to be occupying the entire place. A "No Vacancy" sign along the roadway was illuminated. When Bolan made the scene, only the office cabin was darkened. All others were alight and alive. People were standing around in the rain, exchanging guarded greetings with those in the returning vehicles. A partially clad woman stood framed in the light of an open cabin; another, wearing nothing but panties, was wandering about in the downpour, giggling and singing her greeting. There were perhaps a dozen others in evidence, as well.

A second crew wagon and several other head vehicles were scattered about, parked at the various cabins.

If there was any base security, none was evident. These guys had obviously expected no "trouble" with this assignment. They'd been partying, not warring.

One guy stood out from all the others—a big, mean-looking guy with a Mr. America physique and granite jaw—and, yeah, Bolan knew the guy.

His mental file clicked to an immediate make. Joe Romani was the name, headwhacking was the game—a contract hitman from Boston. He stood now beside the Cadillac, barefoot and clad only in undershirt and trousers, arms folded at the massive chest, conversing loudly with the other crew chief.

"What're you saying, Mario?" Romani rumbled.

"I'm saying your boys pulled me into a suck off, that's what I'm saying," came the taut reply from inside the vehicle.

"How bad are we hurt?"

"Not *we*, Joe. *You*. I brought you two hearses."

Romani stepped back with an angered exclamation and splashed toward an investigation of those "hearses."

The mild excitement of the greeting took a sudden turn toward heated outrage as the base camp revelers began to realize that the hit had gone sour. The dead had friends, yeah, and the friends were mad as hell.

They had been done wrong, sure. Bolan would never cease to marvel at the curious one-way direction in which thought traveled through the Mafia world. That "Turrin bastard" was supposed to meekly hand over his own head to the collectors; maybe he should even thank them for the honor of being executed by his own *amici*. Where the hell did that guy get off, pulling this kind of treacherous shit? The contract was written the other way, dammit. And, yeah—what they would do to Leo the Pussy Turrin for this infamy! He would die by the organ, one of them at a time. He would first drink his own urine and eat his own genitals. Then he would scream and plead for the privilege of dying while his gleeful *amici* taunted and degraded him to the final shuddering breath.

Yeah. Bolan had heard it all before, so many times. It was the logic of savages—and it worked equally well among them all. Today they would together avenge the treachery to their "friends," even though one treachery had begat the other. Tomorrow they could well be the official avengees rather than the avengers—but that all went together with the logic.

That logic was at the heart of the bundle which made Mack Bolan's task so clear-cut. One did not sit down with cannibals and reason with them—not beside their *pots,* at any rate. He had known from the beginning the truth of that rationale. He had known always that there would be a single resolution to the Mafia problem. He had known forever that his would be a terminal war of attrition—a war of absolute obliteration. Death was the only answer these people would ever accept—because it was the only answer they understood.

Mack Bolan was not a cold-blooded man. Nor even an essentially violent one. He could be gentle, if he lived in a gentle world. It was not, however, such a world. Bolan's world was a savage one—and the meek could never hope to inherit such an earth. Not unless the inheritance could be claimed from within a cannibal's bowels.

No. The man was a realist. He knew that the world was doomed to suffer forever in brutality unless the savages could be controlled. He was idealist enough, though, to respect the moral dreams of his society—even though he could not pursue them himself and remain true to his own moral sense. He was thinker enough, also, to wonder if his "own moral sense" was uncomfortably close to the savage logic which he so abhorred.

It was, of course. Close, sure, but not the same.

There was a difference—even if the man himself was, in fact, the only difference. Bolan had probably never heard of Elbert Hubbard, an American writer and lecturer who had died before he was born, but who could have been illustrating the "moral sense" of this twentieth-century American warrior when he proclaimed: "God will not look you over for medals, diplomas, and degrees—but for scars."

If "scars" were what God looked for, then He should have tremendous respect for a man like Mack Bolan.

Bolan himself did not pursue the thought quite that far. In his own mind he knew only that he did what he must do. He knew that he was uniquely equipped to respond to the Mafia challenge to the nobler world—and he knew that he must respond, with his strongest suit. If he picked up scars on the soul along the way—then okay, that was the way it had to be. All of which is not to say that the man never wearied of his burden, never questioned his cause, never wondered whether his response was "wrong," or futile, or both. Bolan was not, in any sense, a superman. He was simply a superb man, with all the dimensions of character that implied.

Right now, yes, he was a wearied and troubled man. The campaign in Georgia—barely twenty-four hours into the past—had been demanding and exhausting. It had been at the height of that campaign that he had discovered the rumbles of "purge" emanating from New York and learned of Leo Turrin's personal jeopardy. He had quickly moved Georgia to an acceptable conclusion and sped forthwith to Pittsfield to find Turrin throwing in the towel and heading for certain destruction—with the directions from Washington so obviously

20

miscalculated to insure that destruction. It was unlike Hal Brognola, the nation's Number One official crimefighter, to be guilty of such erroneous thinking. Bolan had to suspect that the guy was being pressured from somewhere above. If that was true, then the entire Pittsfield stand could already be a futile exercise in the impossible.

Brognola was supposed to be the *only* man in Washington to know the true identity of "Sticker"—Leo Turrin's code name in the undercover ranks. If that cover had been blown in the political malaise that was Washington—then, hell, Leo's game was doomed for sure. And Mack Bolan was therefore engaged in a bloody campaign which could have no meaning whatever in the final tally of things accomplished.

There was no bloodlust in Mack Bolan's makeup.

He did not kill for thrills nor did he make war through any concept of "revenge." He killed because it was the only way to beat the savages—and he made war because, dammit, the savages were winning.

With Leo's life at stake there were, of course, personal considerations—strong enough in themselves to make the battle worthwhile. But there was a larger reason for the Pittsfield stand—and that larger reason bore directly on the overall war effort. Leo Turrin was a highly valuable player in this grim game between the worlds. And, yes, every move mattered. Every good man mattered. Bolan was not being melodramatically cute when he told the Sticker, "I want your *life*, Leo—not your death."

The savages themselves mattered not a damn to Mack Bolan—except in their numbers of dead. He would, sure, kill a million of them if that was what it took to keep one Leo Turrin in the game.

The task was not quite that large, though—at the moment. The task now was to kill but sixteen of the savages.

And they were making it easy for him.

"Get those broads out of here!" Romani yelled, at the top of his voice. "I want a council in ten minutes, *my* cabin! Jake!—Bobby!—you boys get out front and keep the eyes open! Mario!—you come with me right now! I want a complete rundown on this crap!"

"Mario" was obviously the crew boss from Albany. He stepped from his vehicle and angrily slammed the door. "Where do you get off, Joe?" he growled. "Where does it say Boston is running this contract?"

Romani took a menacing step forward and jabbed a stiff finger in the air to punctuate his words as he growled back, "Four dead boys say so, Mario! You want to discuss *that*?"

Albany was not backing down to Boston. The guy thrust his chin forward and sneered, "Yeah, I want to discuss that! It was a suck off! I want to know who was sucking!"

"My four dead boys, maybe," Romani spat disgustedly.

"We both know what staked meat is, Joe! And we both know who staked those boys. They called us into that suck—*they* called it! Maybe we were just closer and got there quicker than anybody expected. Huh?"

Romani preened himself in the falling rain and roared back: "Are you crazy, Mario? Are you clear out of your skull screaming crazy? You saying I set you up for a suck off? To *who*, dammit?"

"To the cops, maybe," Albany raged. "To Leo the Pussy, maybe. How the hell do I know? I just know that I damn near got sucked!"

To that, Romani coldly replied, "If I'd wanted you sucked, guy, you wouldn't be here now complaining about it. Let's go inside and put this thing together. Come on." He turned his back on the Albany leader and went to his cabin.

Mario passed hand-signal instructions to his crew and slowly followed the man from Boston.

The women were being unceremoniously rounded up and ejected from the base camp. They straggled toward several vehicles which were parked at the front of the compound and made their departure without apparent complaint. Professional women, sure—and not locals. The boys would not be that stupid. The women had brought themselves and they were taking themselves away, in their own small caravan.

As the cars departed, one of the guys yelled, "Keep it warm, Marie."

A bare arm waved panties from an open window as the reply sang back: "You'll know where to find it."

The caravan hit the main road and headed east, toward Boston.

Bolan circled immediately to the hastily established forward post and quietly ended the game for the two sentries there—"Bobby" and "Jake," he presumed. He dragged their bodies from the vehicle and deposited them in high weeds alongside the drive, then returned to his own vehicle and prepared for open combat.

He removed his poncho and put it in the trunk of the car, cinched on a readybelt with chest loops, pat-checked the positioning of the various items of ordnance accommodated there, then selected an *Uzi* submachine gun from his mobile arsenal and slung on a belt of spare clips.

He hoped he would not be required to use the explosives—or any other weaponry except the *Uzi*. This was not supposed to bear the marks of an Executioner hit. If he could catch them cold—then okay, yeah, maybe the Uzi would be enough. He had not intended to give them time to settle in, to begin comparing notes and laying reaction plans. The entire camp would almost certainly go "hard" as the first step in that direction. At the moment, the advantage was all his. Within minutes, those odds would begin weighing the other way.

He strode straight along the access road and into the camp. A graves detail was worrying with the corpses of the early dead, moving somberly about in the steady rain and tongue-clucking the unpleasant task as they stacked their dead on a cabin porch. Others stood in small, nervous groups on the porches of other cabins, Boston to the left and Albany to the right, smoking and conversing tensely about the uncertainties of the night.

Bolan was ready to dispel the uncertainties.

He stepped into the open ground between the cabins and found a friendly shadow as he readied the *Uzi* and called out: "Joe! Joe Romani!"

It was time to count bodies, in the opening stand at Pittsfield.

It was no good this way, this tension between the *amici*—and Romani was trying to make that point to the angry shark from Albany, Mario Conti. "It's your contract, Mario," he'd just reminded the guy. "I'm not telling you what to do, or how to do it. I'm just saying that something is haywire. They

24

sent me over here to kiss the guy for you. Okay, I kissed him. The rest is up to you. I just don't like it that four of my boys went down with the kiss. I especially don't like it when you start making dumb noises about a suck off. Something's haywire, that's all."

"Haywire is right," Conti growled. "I was assured it was all set up. I was told it would be a romp. Now I don't know, Joe. I just don't know. I think I want to talk to Albany before anything else. I want to verify the contract."

"That's dumb, Mario," Romani was saying, just as someone outside started yelling his name.

Conti snarled, "What's the matter with those goddamn guys!"

Romani replied, "Ahhh, they can't shit without . . ." He did not finish the sarcasm. Something was wrong outside, definitely wrong.

"Kill that light!" he growled as one of his boys outside replied to the loud summons.

*"Who the hell is that?"*

*"I have a message for Joe from Leo the Pussy!"*

Every one knew the meaning of that. Conti's eyes blanched and skittered away from Romani's startled gaze. The Boston chief leapt to his feet, hit the light switch in one swift motion, and whirled on to the window for a look outside. His boys were all frozen in clutch groups, staring uneasily at something in the darkness beyond the cabins.

Someone nearby yelled, "Joe! Mario! Somebody's here!"

"Stay put!" Romani yelled back. He carefully opened the window and shouted, more loudly: "Who's there? Come into the light and show yourselves!"

Conti had just leapt to the door and cracked it

25

open when a rattling burst from a submachine gun told the tale all had dreaded to hear—and, suddenly, Joe Romani's world fell in on him. That first burst of automatic fire came spiraling into the cabin, punching through the flimsy walls as though no walls existed, disintegrating glass and shredding furniture in an absolutely withering hail that left no cubic volume of air untraveled—and Joe knew that it was all over, right there, in that first stark instant of awareness.

Conti hit the floor with a groan and a bubbling sound at about the same moment that something ripped into Romani's gun arm and spun him around and sent him staggering across the cabin. He fell onto the bed and pulled the shattered arm into his lap, feeling frantically for a pressure point to shut off the flow of blood that was gushing all over him.

His consciousness divided, part of it leaping outside to assess the situation there. It did not sound good out there. The *amici* were returning fire but it sounded disorganized and frantic. Guys were yelling and cussing and running around but the chatter of that chopper went on and on as other guys screamed and called to Jesus in profane prayers.

And suddenly it was over. Impossibly, unbelievably, it was over. He checked an impulse to cry out for help, unsure of just what that sudden silence meant. A moment later he was glad that he'd checked the impulse. The chopper again. Short bursts, widely separated, moving about the yard out there. Romani knew what that meant. It was a clean-up. The chopper was moving among the dying, hastening the process. He shuddered and waited, knowing that his time would come, too weak from shock and pain and bleeding to make a move to save himself.

He heard a movement on the porch, then the door creaked on its hinges and the lights came back on.

The guy was standing outside. He had only reached through the open doorway to switch on the lights. Romani could not see the guy, but he could see the ugly snout of that chopper as fire leapt from it and Mario Conti's bubbling corpse shuddered under the new onslought.

Romani called out, weakly, "Hey! No! Please!"

He was looking up the bore of that chopper—and it was all he could see.

A cold voice said to him from the porch, "Take a message back where you came from, Joe."

"Sure, I'll take the message," Romani groaned hopefully. "Who is that?"

"Never mind who it is. The message is *what* it is. Leopold Turrin does not roll over and die for anybody. Tell them that. And tell them to send *men*, next time."

"Thanks. Thanks. You know what I mean, eh?"

"You know what *I* mean, Romani. You tell them."

"I'll tell them, Leo. Bank on it."

Something sailed through the air and hit the bed beside him. He recoiled, then saw that it was a small first-aid packet.

The snout of the chopper was gone and there were no more sounds from the porch.

Jesus. Jesus God. Had the guy gone? And left Joe Romani alive and with a bandage for his wound? How could you figure it? How the hell could you figure *that*?

Indeed, "the guy" had gone. He was at that mo-

27

ment trudging along the trail toward his vehicle, enveloped by the inner cold that always marked the end of a successful firefight.

Successful, sure. Nineteen bodies, a witness to tell the tale, a note of respect for Leo.

Sure. It was success enough, for a starter. Now the battle would really begin.

# CHAPTER THREE

## Challenged

Joe Romani did not run toward Boston, which was no great surprise to Bolan. Instead, he swung back through Pittsfield and headed north on U.S. 7. The track led to Potter Mountain, then west again into the resort country. The guy was having a hard time of it, moving slowly and weaving somewhat, as, apparently, he fought off the dizzies, halting entirely now and then to collect himself and fight off unconsciousness. Once he got out of the car and walked around it in the rain, the damaged arm in a makeshift sling, slapping his face with a soggy towel to stimulate the fading mind.

Bolan had to respect that effort, even from a savage. The guy was trying; alone and dying, he was still trying.

But it made for a slow track. The total travel was less than twenty miles; the total timetrack was more than an hour. It ended at a secluded mountain resort in the Taconics—a ski lodge, or something similar. Bolan could not positively identify the spot. The sign at the entrance was weathered beyond legibility and the darkness of the rainy night was too complete to allow a quick visual make. It was ski country, however—and the logic seemed to favor an off-season ski lodge. A quick visual make was all he was going to get, this time around. He briefly recalled his Colorado experience and wondered if history might be repeating itself.

Might be, yeah.

The joint sat a couple hundred yards off the road atop a low hill with solid fencing. Rather effectively screened by shrubs and trees, it was a large building with two floors and a high roof—darkened and seemingly deserted. Other shapes loomed nearby in the darkness, suggesting the presence of other, smaller structures.

Romani had pulled onto the access drive—a narrow, asphalt road which snaked up the hill to the compound—where he halted and flashed a recognition signal with his headlamps. An armed patrol in rainslickers appeared immediately to check him out and pass him through.

It was an ominous new development. This was no more "head party" headquarters; it was a hardsite, nothing less—an alien fortress, standing in the heart of Leo Turrin's territory.

Bolan marked the spot in his mind and carefully withdrew. Something big was brewing, that was certain. Something considerably larger, for damn sure, than a routine contract on a small town underboss in a territory nobody had wanted for quite some time.

The game had changed, for sure. To what, though?


Turrin had sent his small personal cadre to bed with orders to "get rested and ready." Then he had withdrawn to his own room in the isolated hideaway and unlocked his "red phone"—the clean line that guaranteed absolute security of communications. At five minutes past each hour, he had attempted contact with Bolan's "floater"—a secure mobile telephone arrangement utilizing a secret access code which tapped into phone company switching facilities. "Secure," that is, as you could get with radio communications. The only security involved was an inability of third parties to track and trace the contacts—the information itself which passed through that contact was subject to intercept-monitoring, and thus required guarded words with shaded meanings.

The system itself, however, was foolproof—as Turrin understood it. Part of the advanced technology built into that fabulous "warwagon"—Bolan's name for the GMC motor home which served the warrior as rolling base camp and battle cruiser—the telephone was indeed a "floater"—in two senses of the word. It "floated" about the country in a highly mobile environment, and it functioned as a remote-controlled answering service for the big impressive man in executioner black—a floater like the kind on a fishing line which signaled a presence on the buried end of that line.

Turrin had been patiently hitting that floater every hour since ten o'clock. His persistence was rewarded at five minutes past the hour of one, when a connection opened and a brusque voice demanded, "Yeah, what's that?"

Turrin grinned as he replied, "It's the Sticker. What's happening, iron man?"

"Plenty," Bolan replied in a noncommittal tone, somewhat relaxing into the contact. "You need to send a message to Augie. Do you have any messengers?"

"Four or five, yeah," Turrin told his friend. "They said they wanted to stay and play. Got something for them to play with?"

"Like I said," the good voice replied, "—a

31

message. Tell me something, first. Have you talked with Augie about the rules of this game?"

"This one? No. I tried. Couldn't get through. What's that message?"

"It has nineteen words," Bolan replied. "You'll find them at the Trails Court on Route 9."

"I know the place. Did you say nineteen words?"

"That's the count. I suggest you put them on ice and send them to your friend."

"Okay," Turrin said thoughtfully. "I think I get the logic but I guess I better get your version of it. Why the refrigerated message?"

"Maybe he doesn't know."

Turrin raised his eyebrows in consideration of that. "You may be right. But I can't bank on it. All the flow seems the other way."

"Either way, he needs the message." That voice had a tired quality. "Flow One says send more and I'll send them back the same way. Flow Two says, what the hell is going on here, Augie? Either way, he needs the message."

"Sure," Turrin replied immediately. "But what if it's Flow One? That would be a red flag in the face, wouldn't it?"

"More like spit," the big guy said, chuckling. "He just may respect that. But I'm leaning toward Flow Two. I let the twentieth word out, just to see where it would lead. And now I have a gut message of my own, Sticker. It does not have Augie's stamp on it."

"Like, what is that?"

"It's like a spanking new hardsite on your doorstep, buddy. Maybe another hundred words just waiting for expression."

Turrin whistled beneath his breath and said, "Which doorstep?"

32

"Toward Albany," was the quiet reply.

"That does not compute," Turrin quickly decided.

"Nothing does, and that's the problem. Send your message, bugler. Let's see what falls from it."

Turrin sighed and said, "Right. We'll try that."

"Play it cozy, though. You know."

"Yeah, I know. I'll safe it."

"Do that. Meanwhile, ease off a bit on the other front. You can forget that dawn deadline. The opposition is jumpy and now not quite so cocksure. They'll safe it along for awhile, also, trying to read the play."

"Should I bet my life on that?"

"I would," Bolan soberly told him.

"That's good enough for me," Turrin replied in the same sober tone.

"Okay," the guy said tiredly. "I'm tucking it away for the night. Haven't slept an hour in the past thirty-six. Try to get that message delivered before daylight. Hit me again at eight o'clock—or before that, if you get some hard flow."

"Will do," Turrin assured him. "I won't even try to say thanks, but—"

"Don't," Bolan growled as the connection went dead.

Turrin stared glumly at the telephone for a thoughtful moment, then put it down and locked it away.

"Some kind of guy," he said aloud.

Then he went to rouse his cadre. They could have a refrigerator truck loaded and ready to roll by two o'clock. A quick jog across the state line and a straight shot down the Taconic State Parkway would place them in New York City by five o'clock.

33

Augie would have his "message" with his morning newspaper—waiting for him at his front door when the new day dawned.

And then, right, oh boy, there would be plenty of "hard flow" for the embattled men at Pittsfield.

That goddamn Mack Bolan was an audacious warrior. Leo Turrin would love to see Augie Marinello's face when he received that shipment of cold meat from western Mass.

Or maybe he wouldn't. No. No. Hell no, he wouldn't.

# CHAPTER FOUR

## Issues and Answers

The special line squawked and squealed, then settled into the familiar, eerie, deep-well tone of the "clean" connection as Harold Brognola's worried voice came through from Washington.

"Okay, it's clear. Go ahead, Sticker. Where are you?"

"Same place," Turrin replied. "It's a new game."

"Says who?"

"Says the Striker. He's on the scene and rattling the cage like crazy. I just sent a ton of damaged meat to New York. I guess that was just a down payment. Striker says there's another five or six tons on site and awaiting collection. That guy is—"

"Out of his mind!" Brognola snarled. "So are you, if you're playing that game. What's it going to look like, Sticker, even if it should work? You can't have that guy romping in there to fight your battles! That's the kiss of death, buddy."

"Relax, Hal. He's playing it cool. No signatures. The guy knows what he's doing. Or should I have to remind you."

The reply came as a resigned sigh. "My orders are to pull you out of there, friend. It's a death trap and we both know it. You've earned your rest. Now come on home."

"Not just yet. Striker cleared me some space to

breathe. I'll stick it awhile longer. He also seems to be thinking toward a whole new game. Something is haywire up here, Hal. Striker says—"

"Striker does not call the plays for this department," Brognola interrupted heavily.

"Who does?" Turrin quietly inquired.

Another tired sigh, then: "Maybe I deserve that. Okay. Go on. What's haywire?"

"I don't know, for sure. Neither does Striker, at the moment, but he's sniffing—and the odor he reports is mighty peculiar. We sent that meat to Augie, Hal. Striker is—"

"That guy is death looking for a place to happen! We've known that all along, haven't we. Don't be there when the happening arrives, Sticker. You can't go taunting the old bosses that way. Get out. Right now. Let the guy pull the home town down around his ears, if he must, and let the happening happen. I can't play this game any longer. Neither can you. It started there for him, okay, so maybe he has a special interest. Fine. Let it end there, if it must. For him, though—not for you!"

"That's mighty goddamned cozy talk, isn't it," Turrin chopped back bitterly. "A fine goddamned pair we would be, wouldn't we. Why don't we just reverse the clock, Hal. Turn it back to start. Where were *you* then, buddy? Where was I? Put the Striker in the grave that was dug for him in that beginning, then send us on our way alone. Where are we now? I'm probably long dead, buried, forgotten—a quiet notation in a secret book consigned to some time capsule in the Department of Justice. You're a vague name that nobody can pronounce, beating your brains against the combine in one futile field operation after another. You can't play *this* game, Hal? What the hell game *can* you play?"

"Okay, okay. I just—"

"Okay, *hell!* The guy has given us both every damned thing we are at this minute. Don't sit there at the top of your fancy new bureaucracy and tell me you can't play the game!"

"Okay, dammit, okay—I surrender! For Christ's sake!"

"Okay," Turrin growled.

"I was simply trying to be pragmatic," the Justice Department official added defensively.

"Oh, sure."

"The heat is up and you know it. This goddamn town has become impossible. I have people walking up and down my back from Capitol Hill to the goddamn Pentagon and twice around the White House. Don't make me alibi beyond that."

"Just leave off the pragmatic bullshit, eh?"

"All right. I apologize. Does that smooth your ruffled feathers? It doesn't alter the truth of what I said. The guy is pounding sand in Pittsfield. The territory is gone. If you want to help the guy, then convince him of that. Then both of you write it off and get the hell out while you can."

"What do you know that I don't, Hal?"

"Nothing for sure."

"Has my cover been compromised in Washington?"

"There is that possibility," Brognola replied, sighing.

"I don't buy enigmatic bullshit either, buddy. Is it or isn't it?"

"In the sense of a positive ID—no, of course not. But there *has* been a leak, of sorts. Some people up in the Senate are digging like crazy. It's all part of this domestic intelligence flap we've been going through."

Turrin felt a cold hand at his heart. "How bad is it, Hal?"

"Bad enough. I'm under a Senate subpoena, right now. They already know that we have a sticker. They suspect that he may be actually running an organized crime family. And some of them may be uncomfortable with the thought that the U.S. government is officially subsidizing a—"

"That's dumb!" Turrin snarled. "Anybody with half a mind knows that the mob cannot exist unless some key people in government are playing ball. If they want to be uncomfortable, why don't they go after the made men in Washington—or in New York or Chicago or in the various state houses around this pragmatic country! Don't tell me—!"

"That's not the point and you know it's not," Brognola tiredly interrupted. "You can't ask a politician to think in a straight line—especially not during an election year. The issue is morality in government, *official* government, and how many politicos have you ever met who can talk in anything but circles when it comes down to election-year issues? A target is a target—and, right now, yours truly seems to be it."

Turrin sighed into the connection. "Why do I get the feeling—every time you mention politics—that I'm going to lose an argument? I get new respect for Striker every day. His answer is best. His answer is to *no one* in government."

He heard the snap of a lighter and knew that the troubled man at the other end of that connection was lighting a cigar. A good man, sure—but a particularly bedeviled one, at this curious time of gov-

38

ernmental tensions. Turrin's anger was directed not at the man, but at the forces moving that man.

Brognola's voice, when it rejoined the conversation, was contrite and controlled. "You haven't lost anything, good buddy. You're right and I'm wrong. I have a date this afternoon before the Senate subcommittee. I'm going to tell those worried gentlemen to go straight to hell. It's your job, and it's your game. No one can call the shots but you. Do it."

"Thanks. Watch your swinger, Hal."

"I'll do that. I'll keep it tucked in close. But listen to me, Sticker. There's ungodly pressure bearing on this situation. And our friend the Striker is probably one hundred percent right. It smells. The odor has nightmarish suggestions."

"Uh huh. Striker has made note of the many tabs in Washington. He seems to think we could see the moment when congressmen are doubling as hitmen."

"Like I said," Brognola replied noncommittally, "—nightmarish suggestions."

"You agree, then."

"Sure I agree. What d'you think I've been—?"

"Enough said, then."

"Right. Tell Striker to give them one for me. But don't look this way for any realistic help. Right now I am walking a tightrope. I could be fired or jailed or both by the next nightfall. Meanwhile I'll be standing by for all the quiet support I can offer. But that's the best I can do."

"I understand. Get in touch with, uh, your liaison in Pittsfield. Tell him what is going down and ask for his quiet cooperation."

"With regard to Striker?"

"In that regard, yeah. It's the quiet game, Hal.

39

We just don't want any advertising—not right away. You know what I mean."

"I know, yeah. Okay. End of conversation?"

"I guess so. Oh, uh, get word to Angie. Tell her I'm riding it through awhile longer. Tell her—no, don't tell her anything. Just explain the change in plans—so she won't be worrying when I don't show up."

"Right. Gutsy little lady you have there, Sticker. Not many could handle the life. She handles it very well."

"Yeah. Let her know, eh?"

"You know I will."

The connection vanished and Leo Turrin sat back to ponder the various nuances of that furtive conversation.

Nightmarish, eh?

So what was new? The "life" was an unending, living nightmare.

He went to the window to check the eastern horizon for evidence of a new day. Not yet. Soon, though, a pragmatic new day for morality in America would present itself at that horizon.

What a hell of a bitter joke that was!

Thanks—but no, thanks. Leo Turrin would stick to Mack Bolan's answers to the issue. He would stick, if necessary, all the way to the grave.

# CHAPTER FIVE

## First Light

First light was just cracking the night skies above the impressive Long Island estate when Billy Gino, the security boss, ran up the winding stairway to the porch and presented himself at the TV camera.

"Trouble," he reported quietly. "Let me in."

The door buzzed and opened itself.

"Is David there?" he asked the houseman as he stepped inside.

The guy nodded and said, "Where else."

"There" was the morning room—a bay-windowed breakfast nook at the east side of the house. David Eritrea, personal secretary and "business manager" to the aged and infirm lord of the manse, was an habitual early riser. Some of the housemen claimed that the guy never slept—that they heard his footsteps moving around upstairs all night long, that his habitual orange juice and toast with the rising sun was not an awakening discipline but merely the long-awaited end to a lonely night.

Old man Marinello, it was said, was subject to terrifying nightmares. House talk had it that the faithful Eritrea crept about in the night only so as to be on hand to awaken the boss and soothe him in such moments. It had been that way since that terrible night in Jersey when Mack the Bastard blew the old man in half with a grenade.

41

The security chief found Eritrea in his customary spot, seated at the window, with the customary breakfast before him. A classy guy—he always looked the same, sounded the same, acted the same. A bit prissy, maybe—but no one had ever said so to his face.

"Good morning, Billy," Eritrea greeted him. "What evil is bursting from that worried head on such a fine morning?"

The guy was uncanny. He could pick up mental vibes, Billy was certain of that. Nobody ever before had been able to read the security chief's poker face.

"Somebody abandoned a truck on the front drive," Gino reported quietly. "No one saw it or heard it come up. One minute it wasn't there. Next minute it was."

Eritrea stared at him for a moment before replying, "So call the police and have it hauled away."

"It's not, uh—I don't think we want that."

"We don't want that?"

"No, sir. I sent a boy to check it out. It's a refrigerator van. Carrying a load of meat."

Eritrea raised the orange juice to his lips and murmured, "So?"

"Human meat."

The cool bastard drained the glass of juice and lit a cigarette before replying, "Okay. Better bring it inside, eh."

Gino nodded and started to leave when Eritrea called him back.

"Billy. Have the powder men check it out first. Stay away until they give it a clean bill."

"Yes, sir, I'll do that."

"Then send for Barney Matilda and his crew. I

42

want him to handle it. Tell him I'll expect a full report within the hour."

"He lives about twenty minutes away, Mr. Eritrea. That doesn't give—"

"Within the hour, Billy."

The security chief acknowledged the instructions and hurried away.

*Within the hour,* sure. It wasn't as easy as downing a glass of orange juice, David. It wasn't even full daylight yet. Within the hour, eh. Call out the bomb squad, call out the garbage detail and ID specialists, get a complete make on the vehicle and its grisly contents, and bring it all back in a nice neat package *within the hour.*

Okay. That was what David wanted. As usual, that was what David was going to get.

The full task actually required some fifty-five minutes. Barney Matilda was a semi-retired senior citizen who'd been down many bloody roads with old man Marinello—and he was still the best cleanup man in the business.

Billy Gino accompanied the old guy to the upstairs sitting room where Marinello customarily held court, and they sat there in awkward silence staring at each other for several minutes before Eritrea came in.

"How's Augie?" Barney immediately inquired.

"Best sleep he's had all night," Eritrea reported with a soft voice and a commanding look. "He always sleeps best at first light. Let's see that he enjoys it. What do we have here, Barney?"

"Some kind of war, I'd guess," the old guy replied. "But I can't figure why they'd send the garbage to us. Nineteen boys, David. All died about the same time, I'd say, give or take an hour. All of them were gunshot. More than one weapon did the killing, of course. Thirty-twos and thirty-eights, looks like—dum-dum slugs. The thirty-eights did a lot of tearing and shredding, more than they had a right to. High-powered charges, maybe—a Luger type or something like that—magnums, maybe."

"Did you get some identity?"

"I couldn't make them all. You'll have to wait for fingerprint ID for the full story there. A day or so, I'll rush it through. But I made a few Boston boys. And I made a few Albany boys. Arm and leg men, David. Contract specialists."

"*All* of them?"

"All of them we made, yeah. I'll have something more definite later today. I mean connections, you know."

"What about the truck?"

"Very interesting truck. Belongs to a packing house in Springfield, Massachusetts. Has their decals two feet high on both sides. Guy up there says it went to Pittsfield yesterday afternoon on an overnight turnaround. I left it at that. It's legit. There's no key in the ignition. It's been hotwired."

"Pittsfield, eh," Eritrea commented thoughtfully. "That's only an hour or so from Albany, isn't it? You figure someone skipped into Massachusetts and snatched a truck just to set this up?"

The old man shook his head. "Doesn't figure that way, David. I think they wanted us to know for damn sure where the truck came from. I think someone sent us a message. I just can't figure why. Can you?"

Eritrea grinned suddenly. That was bad. From personal and intimate experience, Billy Gino knew that was bad.

"Get the garbage out of here," the guy said coldly.

"I'll send it to the rendering plant."

"Whatever, just do it and do it right. Soon as you have a full rundown, I want it. That means names and affiliations, the whole bag. You know what to do with the truck."

"Yeah. We'll cycle it through."

"Billy!"

"Yes, sir."

"This one gets the silent treatment."

"Oh yes, sir."

"Make sure everybody understands. We'll never hear of this again, will we."

"I already forgot what we were talking about, Mr. Eritrea."

"That means you, too, Barney."

The old guy waved his hand in dismissal of the ridiculous. "Oh, sure."

"Double security around here, Billy, until I say different. Nobody comes and nobody goes without my knowledge."

"Yes, sir."

"Send the house boss up here on your way out. And tell Nick I'll be going to the city in thirty minutes. I'll want full security for that trip. Get the cars ready."

The guy stood up. That meant goodbye. Billy Gino leapt to his feet and took old Barney by the arm just in case the guy hadn't got that message.

"Give Augie my best," the old fellow requested as he was being led away.

"I'll tell him you were here," Eritrea said solemnly.

Matilda looked at Gino and back again to Eritrea. "Tell him I'd like to see him. It's been a long time. Tell him I—"

"He was asking about you just yesterday," Eritrea said softly. He smiled. "Told me a very funny story about you and Charley Lucky on the Atlantic Pier."

The old man beamed and allowed himself to be gently hauled from the room. As they were descending the stairs to the main level, though, those shrewd old eyes threw a parting glance toward that upstairs room as he asked Billy Gino, "When's the last time you saw Augie?"

"I see him every day," the security boss lied, then wondered why he'd done that.

"I haven't seen him since just before the Montreal meet," Barney complained.

Billy Gino was still wondering. When *was* the last time he'd seen the boss? "David runs this joint, now," he told the old man.

Crafty eyes flashed at him. "David may be running more than you think, Billy boy."

Gino chuckled at that, but only to cover his own wandering thoughts. "David has been Augie's good right man for a long time," he reminded the oldster. "I guess since the accident he's had to be his legs, too. Don't you worry none about Augie Marinello, Barney. Not while David is around. They're just like father and son."

The old man gave him an odd look and went on to the door alone.

Billy Gino wandered back to the kitchen. Cookie was bustling around back there, preparing breakfast for the thirty-odd-man staff and complaining about the mess of dirty cups and pastry crumbs left by the night crew.

"How has Augie been eating lately?" the security chief idly inquired while pouring himself some coffee.

"Good as ever," Cookie snapped.

"How good is that?" Gino persisted.

"Little here, little there. He's been a sick man, Mr. Gino."

"How sick?"

"You know what I mean."

"No, I'm trying to find out what you mean. How sick is he?"

The cook's eyes darted about the kitchen for a moment as though he were about to divulge a big secret, then he said, "You'd better ask Mr. Eritrea about that."

"I'm asking you, Cookie."

"Look. Ask the doctor. He's here every day. Ask *him*."

"Are you feeding him or aren't you?"

"He's been on a special diet for more than a month."

The guy walked away and busied himself at the refrigerator.

Billy Gino doggedly followed him.

"How special?"

"Very special. Aw, come on, Mr. Gino. Don't put me on the spot. Don't put me in the middle of this. Mr. Eritrea would skin me alive if . . ."

Billy Gino snapped, "Forget it," and went out of there. He had to roust Nick and the bodyguard crew for a secure caravan run to Manhattan. It wasn't all that unusual, hell no, but with everything else that had come with first light . . .

And he thought he knew, now, why David Eritrea walked the floor all night every night in that upper sanctuary where no one else was permitted. Augie Marinello was dying. They were probably keeping the old boy alive with tubes and bottles, hope and prayer.

47

That was too bad, sure—but why the big dark secret?

Why not take the old man to the hospital and give him a medical chance? Or was it that hopeless? And were they all scared to death that the empire would die with him? A lot of people, sure, had been waiting a long time for Augie Marinello to die. Ambitious people, sharkish people.

And what did that shipment of cold meat, delivered at the doorstep at first light, have to do with all this? A message of some sort, no doubt about that. Old Barney had been wondering about it. David had apparently figured it out.

Billy Gino shivered and went on to his duties.

A new day had dawned. And Billy knew somehow that things would never again be the same for the Marinello Family.

They had not been the same, indeed, since that terrible night in Jersey when Mack the Smasher had made half a man out of the boss of bosses. Now the other half was dying. And the empire, apparently, was coming apart at the seams.

Was the fine hand of Mack Bolan at work again?

He hoped not. Billy Gino sure as hell hoped for anything but that. He made a run for the front door, suddenly vividly aware that he needed to talk to old Barney Matilda. Barney was the master craftsman—the ultimate cleanup man—and old Barney would know.

Barney had cleaned up behind Mack Bolan a couple times before. Even, yeah, after that terrible night in Jersey.

48

# CHAPTER SIX

## Outside In

The rain had ended during the night and the skies were mostly clear. The warwagon was parked along the shore of Pontoosuc Lake, at the city's northwest edge. The view through the one-way window took Bolan briefly back through the years, to happier times and to those occasional camping trips with his dad—the sun peeking over those same Berkshire Hills, the smell of bacon cooking in the crisp, morning air.

The memories were there, yeah, but fleeting and elusive, hard to capture and embrace with anything more than a tendril of the mind. Most of Mack Bolan's memories, now, were of the other life. They were visions of war and survival, blood and death and terror—lessons learned the hard way—and he recognized that this was the way it must be, for a survival candidate.

So he shrugged away the wispy echoes of a kinder past and turned his energies to work toward survival in an uncertain future. A dreadful future, maybe, sure—but he reminded himself that it was the only one available.

He showered, shaved, and donned appropriate clothing for the day ahead, then had a quick breakfast and put the day into motion. The Ford sedan which had carried him about the city during the night was now under tow by the warwagon. The big Toronado power plant was not even aware of the extra load as it smoothly pushed the battle cruiser through the hills. Thanks to a remote console arrangement forward in the con, the computerized plotting board of the amidships console was feeding him terrain information and topographical maps of the entire western edge of Massachusetts and eastern New York state. The slowly moving display gave him plenty of time to absorb the details and still give proper attention to navigation as he invaded that enemy territory.

A "sector view" occupied and overlay an upper corner of the viewscreen, relating his own position and movement through another computerized system of navigational vectoring. The electronics were positively awesome, and Bolan had not yet ceased to marvel at their effectiveness. The systems had come to him with the compliments of an aerospace wizard in New Orleans, who, after the installation, had proudly advised the new owner: "You've got everything the space program can apply to your problem, Mr. Striker."

So much for space-age technology, in a world intent upon eating itself. It helped, of course—but it also made Bolan's war larger, and, thus, more complicated. To offset the wider reach, he also needed wider combat capabilities. So another wizard provided the latest in communications and intelligence-gathering technology; yet another, the ultimate in weaponry and electronic fire control. It had cost a pile of money, sure. All of it came from the warchest, though, which itself was kept stocked by involuntary contributions from the enemy's own flow of black bucks—so it worked out rather well, with the mob supplying its greatest enemy with the cash needed to fuel the machinery of its own destruction. Bolan thought that particularly fitting —justice in all its poetic sense.

At the moment, though, the skipper of the warwagon was thinking only of getting inside that new enemy hardsite in the Berkshire Hill country of western Mass and learning its secrets. The single most important task of the moment, in that regard, involved an intimate familiarity with the territory itself. Bolan's memories of the area were mostly childhood perceptions. They would not serve him well, now. What he needed was a soldier's familiarity, and that was precisely what he was acquiring via the warwagon's fantastic technologies.

He devoted a couple of hours to prowling the backroads and trails, taking careful note of the various terrain features and committing them to the personal combat computer within his own skull—relating them to human habitation, commercial establishments and activities, transport routes, communications and power transmission lines, waterways—the entire "lay"—from all of which he meticulously selected the site for his forward base and began preparations for a penetration of the enemy camp.

"Penetration" did not necessarily entail the injection of a physical human body across enemy lines. All that was required, to get the outside inside and the inside outside, was to inject the *human senses* into the situation—and that was what the warwagon was all about.

He'd located the perfect site. The enemy was below and within range of the optic systems—unwind, barring a sudden shift, and that would be a plus for the audio effort—sufficiently distant so as to not arouse suspicions which could defeat the surveillance. For a special added factor, the telephone lines serving the hardsite were a mere hundred yards away.

As the first order of business, Bolan activated the optics and programmed the video recorders for "movement-actuated" service. There would be no simple landscape or still-life scenes recorded. Only motion of a particular type would trigger the system and commit the action to a video recording.

Next, he focused the barrel-mike pickups for the audio surveillance systems, positioning two of them for wide-angle pickup and zeroing—in a third "hi-sense" mike on an open window at the side of the target building. He set a low threshold for the sound-actuated recorders, crossed his fingers, and went on to the next important step.

This one was a bit trickier. It was not space-age technology but Bell System basics which had to be applied here, and he tapped into a half-dozen carriers, using a simple but effective process of elimination, before striking paydirt. And there was but one way to be sure of that.

He got a surly response from the first ring: "Club Taconic."

"I want to make a reservation," Bolan told the guy.

"No way, buddy, too bad—we're closed for the season."

"Are you sure?" Bolan inquired, a bit belligerently.

"Whattaya mean, am I sure? Sure I'm sure."

"Well, maybe I have the wrong place. I'm supposed to be meeting my girl there. How the hell am I going to—?"

"That's your problem, buddy." The guy seemed to be enjoying the problem just the same. "What-

52

taya mean, you don't even know where you're supposed to be? Do you even know where you're *at*?"

The guy was bored and looking for a bit of diversion—and he had a sadistic humor, as well—all of which was just fine with Bolan. He faked a nervous laugh as he told the guy: "I guess I better come up there, just the same. Rosalie must have goofed. When she shows up—listen, she's a tall—"

"Hey hey, hold it! I told you we're closed. Nobody comes. Got it? If the broad shows, she'll be turned away at the gate by the security people. You got the wrong place, guy. Try over there in the public ski area—what's it called?—Jiminy Cricket or something."

"Jiminy Peak?" Bolan corrected him. "Isn't that where you are located?"

"Naw, hell naw, Jesus Christ! I hope you make out better with Rosalie, dum dum. You want me to go over there and lead you to the right hole, guy?"

Bolan muttered, "Sorry," and removed his patch.

But he was not at all sorry. He taped a microtransceiver to the pole and made the connection, then returned to the warwagon and set up the voice-actuated monitor.

He was inside them, now. More than that—he was like a ghost, all over them—watching, listening—getting their form, fit, and function.

Soon, now—the fates willing—he would know what to do with them. But the question was no longer an "if"—it was now only *what* and *when*.

Right now, it was time for a talk with Leo.

Those guys were getting too bored, down there. It was time for a bit of outside stimulation.

He took the 8:05 contact on the floater and told his friend, "We need a plain language line. Give

53

me a number, and make sure it's clean. I'll call you back in five minutes."

Turrin complied without comment. Five minutes later, Bolan was up the pole again with another patch.

"Okay, it's cleared for plain language," Turrin told him.

"Have you had any dialogue with New York yet, Leo?"

"Nothing that counts, no. I've been hitting Augie every twenty minutes for the past two hours. All I can get is the house boss, and he's putting no calls through. Sounds like they're on full alert."

"Do you personally know that house boss?"

"Sure. Guy named de Florio. Been with the old man for years. He's friendly enough when I call. He just says his orders are that the old man cannot be disturbed. And he claims that Augie's good right hand is not available for calls."

"Who is that good right hand? Eritrea, still?"

"That's the guy. He's been sort of running things for Augie the past few months."

"What are your feelings there?"

"Eritrea? Damned good man. I wish he was mine."

"He's one of the new guard, right?"

"Right. Educated and polished. Took over for Augie as *consigliere* after a background in Columbia business school and a later stint with the *Commissione*. Very bright, and much harder inside than the outside might reveal."

"Yeah, I have the guy," Bolan commented. "You figure he's entirely loyal to Augie, eh."

"I honestly can't feel that one out, Sarge. I just don't know. He's not the sort of guy you get next to, if you know what I mean."

54

"You figure your message of the dawn got through okay?"

"For sure, yeah. I managed to get through to my man in Manhattan—and he was almost too nervous to talk to me."

"Did you get the leper feeling?"

"Oh absolutely. The word is out, that's for sure."

"This is the guy that works for the *Commissione*?"

"Same guy, right. He says the town is uptight and I shouldn't be calling around this way. They got my message out on Long Island, yeah, for sure. My man says some hot sparks got ignited out there early this morning. Says a full council has been requested, via Augie. They should be meeting about now."

"Yeah, that's very interesting," Bolan said. "Tell me about this 'man' of yours. What's his fit?"

"Well, you know how it works. Sort of like White House staff, aides and such. A lot of people take care of the routine business for the organization. Naturally, everybody wants to cultivate and con these guys as much as possible. It's a link, you know, a tie to the top. My guy is one of those links."

"He's just a contact, though. He hasn't been made by you."

"Well, in a way, yeah, he has. We all do that and everyone knows it. It's the way the game is played."

A brief silence ensued while Bolan thought about that. Then he observed, "But nobody knows for sure which man is yours."

"You got it. It couldn't work any other way."

"So this guy is really in a dangerous spot, if word should get out that you've made him."

"That's an understatement, Sarge. The best could

happen to him, he'd be sent to Arizona or New Mexico. In the mob, that's the equivalent of Siberia."

"Okay," Bolan said thoughtfully. "We need to rattle some cages, Leo. You're going to have to go public."

The little guy sighed across the connection as he replied, "Yeah, I'm way ahead of you. I already sent out a roundup call. My boys will be drifting back into town, right about now. They also will be bringing as many friends as they can collect along the way. The numbers should be, oh, say forty guns at the best. Half of those will be amateurs. You know what I mean."

Bolan replied, "Yeah."

How well he knew what Leo meant. Street punks with no allegiance to anything but a quick buck, willing to do anything to anybody if the price was right. The major problem there was that their ambitions greatly exceeded their capabilities. Strong on talk but weak on delivery. Dreamers, these guys, who imagined themselves as big bad men until they found themselves in the midst of a firefight.

Bolan knew precisely what Leo meant. He said, "The show of arms is what's important. You know the risks, buddy. There will be plenty of heat."

"So what's new?" the little fed replied. "Exactly what do you want me to do? I don't want to know your gameplan. Just tell me what I do to mesh with it."

Bolan chuckled. "Superstitious?"

"Naw, just sensible. If I fall, I don't want you falling with me."

"The gameplan, Leo, is to keep you upright. So

56

let's keep that goal up front. Everything else has to play to it. Tell me you understand that."

Turrin gave a hollow laugh. "I understand it. And I'd be a liar or a fool to say that I don't appreciate the goal. What do I do, then?"

"Fit yourself into a strong defensive position— something you know you can hold. Then start making your noises and dare them to send you some more trouble. Make sure you're covered in every possible area. No weaknesses, nothing hanging out. Then start yelling and sit tight."

"Got it. Okay. Sounds easy enough. You're expecting me to play some dirty pool, too, I take it. You're thinking about my man in Manhattan."

Bolan sighed. "Yeah. You're going to have to expose the guy, Leo. Load him up, then cut him loose. I'm sorry if—"

"No no, it's okay. The guy would do the same to me. Please note that I did not give away my position when I talked to him this morning. In a society of thieves, Sarge, you just don't—"

Bolan broke in with a laugh, then told him, "Okay, Leo. You know what you have to do. I want some waves, high and fierce. Cover yourself and start your move. Right now."

"Right now, okay, you've got yourself a wave-making machine. Just don't get caught in the undertow, buddy."

Bolan chuckled solemnly and rang off.

He was not particularly concerned about his place in undertows. It was, indeed, the best way he knew for getting the outside in and the inside out.

And that was the whole damn gameplan.

# CHAPTER SEVEN

## Shaking It

Billy Gino dropped off at the end of the ramp with two of his boys and watched with customary nervousness as the other cars swept past and nosed into their parking spots.

Everything was moving with the usual precision.

Four of the boys were hustling along the corridors while another pair quickly checked out the elevator area and sent back an all clear. Only then did David and his entourage disembark and flow swiftly across to the elevators.

Gino remained behind to put his personal seal of security on the parked vehicles. He called the wheelmen together for the routine instructions: "Stick close. Keep your butts off the floor and your ears and eyes open. Don't let nobody near the cars. I'll beep you when we start down. You have it hot and ready to roll when we come out of those elevators."

He told the other downstairs boys: "Keep it casual but keep it tight. Anything at all bothers you, give me a beep." He hauled out his little pocket radio, turned it on, and clipped it to his belt. "Let's have a radio check when I get upstairs."

Then he went on up, fighting the usual quivers within himself. It was always a nervous job—especially when they were "on the town." Billy Gino was getting paid for his nerves. And he earned his pay. He was a good bodycock and he took his work seriously. Somehow, though, today the tensions were even worse than usual. Something was in the air—something ominous and worrisome—and a good security boss always respected those backbone shivers. Not that he suspected some sort of ambush and shootout right here in midtown Manhattan—not, anyway, right here under *La Commissione*'s exalted noses. But a guy had to be ready for the unsuspected. And something definitely was off key with the organization. Something was happening, and Billy Gino did not understand what that was, and his bodycock's nerves were paying the price for that confusion.

He stepped off the elevator and into the foyer of the penthouse, re-positioned a couple of his boys there for better separation from the other contingents, and snapped at them: "Don't mingle. Don't yap. Stay alert." Then he checked the radio. These big buildings had a lot of steel. Communications were never as good as Billy would have preferred. He always checked the radios when they came here—and he was never entirely satisfied with the results, although he had never, in his memory, really needed to use the damn things in this particular location.

It had never occurred to Billy Gino that the entire world did not conduct its business in this fashion. He had never even thought about it. This was the way it was—top security, peaking nerves, ugly suspicions, and guns never more than a fingerflick away. This was the way it had always been, the way it always would be. There were no other worlds.

He went on into the big lounge area which was off limits to all but ranking officers of the company and their personal men. The place was patrolled by frozen-faced steeleyes in hand-tailored threads who sort of blended into the decor like so many pieces of animated furniture. These were the *Commissione's* own men, a gestapo elite without family ties or divided loyalties. They served no boss in particular, rather, they were responsible to all as to a corporate body—they served an idea, not a man. Or, so it was said. Billy had never liked those guys. He had never really trusted them. Today, he trusted them even less.

One of them approached and spoke to him, as if from some loudspeaker concealed under the coat, no expression in the face or eyes, no movement of lips or jaws—a damned ventriloquist. "How goes it on Long Island, Billy?"

"It goes fine, thanks," the bodycock replied, in much the same manner.

"I hear you got some funny flesh out there this morning."

"Where'd you hear that?" Billy Gino replied casually and strolled on past the guy.

David was waiting for him near the door to the council chamber. The security chief moved alongside to deliver his report. "It looks okay, Mr. Eritrea. But I have a nervous feeling."

"So have I, Billy," David replied quietly.

That surprised Billy Gino. Not that the guy felt that way—but that he had confided it to his bodycock. He had never known David Eritrea to reveal any feeling to anyone.

They went inside and Billy went through the usual quiet routine of checking the place out while

David exchanged restrained greetings with the other men assembled there. The protocol was immaculate. David was not even a boss, yet he was the last to enter and he sat at the head of the table. In this chamber, David was not David; he was Augie Marinello—a walking and talking extension of the boss of bosses.

Billy Gino caught his eye with a silent "okay" and went back out to take up station immediately beyond the heavy door. That station was his prerogative, as bodycock to the boss of bosses. It was an unwritten and even an unspoken prerogative, but it was there, nevertheless, and Billy Gino exercised it. Not even the steeleyes could challenge his right to stand at that closed door. Nobody better, either.

Tensions, yeah—they were so heavy you could feel them gritting between your teeth. What the hell was going on?

A steeleye approached, acting like he was going right through the door past Billy Gino. Billy impaled him with a what-the-hell look, and the guy came to a quick halt.

"Where the hell you think you're going?" the bodycock softly inquired.

"Message for Mr. DiAnglia," steeleye explained, without really seeming to say anything.

Billy pointed to the house phone on a table nearby. "So send it," he said.

He would have none of that shit.

The guy slid over to the phone and sent the message inside to DiAnglia, lord of the Bronx and Staten Island too. The conversation was exceedingly brief and hardly rose above a whisper, but Billy distinctly heard the word "Pittsfield."

Steeleyes went away as quietly as he'd come, like a damn slithering snake.

Billy Gino stood at the door for another ten minutes, fidgeting inside and wondering about the contents of that "Pittsfield" message. Then the door opened, and David was there.

"Send for Angelo Flavia," David commanded, then shut the door.

Flavia was one of the "executives" whose offices were on the floor below the penthouse. Billy raised a hand and a steeleye immediately drifted over. "They want Flavia," he told the guy.

A minute later, they had Flavia.

He was a guy of about forty, fat and smooth and soft all over, a typical headquarters boy who probably lived in a fancy eastside highrise, spent his evenings at the Playboy Club, got a manicure and haircut twice a week, and spent the rest of his time trying to figure ways to increase his stock in the company. Billy had never had a very high opinion of these headquarters types. They were so many parasites clinging to the body of the work which every day was being gouged out of those streets far below—which work these guys would not touch even with leather gloves to protect their dainty, manicured paws.

Billy knocked lightly on the door and took the guy inside.

"Stay, Billy," David commanded.

Billy Gino stayed, closing the door and planting himself against it from the inside.

Flavia was nervous as hell. The old bosses just sat there, staring at him. David was at the window. He turned to the guy and softly asked him, "How are things in Pittsfield, Angelo?"

The guy threw a sick look at Billy Gino, then put his knuckles on the table and leaned on them as he told Eritrea, "I haven't been hearing much from Pittsfield, David."

"That's not the way I get it," Eritrea said coldly.

"I don't know what—look, really, what are you saying?"

"Flat out I'm saying that we know about you and Leo the Pussy," Eritrea said, not unkindly. "We have a bad situation here, Angelo. We have to think that we can count on you to keep the loyalties unscrambled. Is that unreasonable?"

The guy was almost strangling on his own words as he replied, "It's not a *question* of loyalties, David. I just—hell, I'm in a bad spot. I heard about the funny flesh out your way this morning, sure. That sort of thing naturally worries me. I'm trying to find out what's going down, that's all. Sure, I've had a few drinks with Leo. Seemed like an all right guy. But shit I'm not in the guy's pocket. You ought to know better than that. If there's anything at all I can do to straighten all this out, of course you can count on me. You have to know that."

Eritrea's eyes were saying precisely *what* he knew, but the voice was easier on the guy. "Now's your chance to prove it," he observed softly.

"Can I sit down?" the guy asked, already moving toward a chair as he spoke.

And, sure, that was a good idea. Another second and the guy would have been kneeling on the floor.

Eritrea gave the look to Billy Gino. The bodycock nodded solemnly and went back to his station outside the door.

Things were looking better. A lot better. And old man Marinello would have been quite proud of David if he could have seen him now.

The meeting dissolved a short while later. The bosses drifted out, looking solemn and troubled. David came out with a hand on Angelo Flavia's shoulder. Things looked pretty cozy between them. But the guy was still sweating it. He was sweating it hard. Billy Gino knew why, too—he'd seen David Eritrea work on a guy like this many times in the past.

"Call the airport, Billy," David instructed in a quiet aside to his bodycock. "Get the company plane ready for a run to Pittsfield. We'll be leaving within the hour."

"Him, too?" Billy Gino sniffed with a jerk of the eyes toward the sweating Flavia.

David almost smirked. "Bet your ass, him too," he snarled.

Billy went to the telephone and made the call.

Things were looking better, for damn sure. It had all been in a slow slide to hell ever since Jersey. It was long past time for the company to shake itself—and it sure was good to have a whole man running the show again, no disrespect to Augie intended.

The bodycock had long known what was now being whispered everywhere in the organization.

David Eritrea was a whole man and a half. Boss or no boss, he was sure as hell running the show now.

And Billy Gino could hardly wait to see the fur start flying. His nervousness had evaporated. He supposed that it had been produced in the first place by an uneasiness over that Bolan bastard. Old Barney Matilda had said nothing to ease the mind on that score. "Doesn't have the marks of a typical Bolan hit," the old guy had muttered. "But you never can tell. With that guy, you never know."

Billy Gino still did not know. But it did not seem to matter, now. No. It really did not matter now.

# CHAPTER EIGHT

# Fire Mission

It was precisely the sort of development Bolan had been angling for and it came whispering across the telephone monitor in hushed and guarded language.

"Club Taconic."

"This is Peter. Tell Simon, please."

"Yes, sir. One minute."

Biblical names, again—shades of Atlanta.

A moment later, from the strong side of the connection: "We were wondering how you've been and why we haven't heard for so long."

"Sorry. We've had a busy time. Is it cool there?"

"Cool enough, yes. How is your weather?"

"Warming up rather quickly, Simon. There's been, uh, some confusion in the marketplace."

"Didn't you get our bid? We put in a sell order."

Bolan had his head cocked toward the monitor, straining to read voice characteristics and getting nothing but soft sibilance and unemotional courtesies.

The weak side was replying: "It came too late for positive action. Sorry. Another seller cornered the market with a dump price. Haven't you heard?"

"We've heard nothing," said the whispers from the hardsite. "We have not exactly been listening.

Concerns with internal communications, you know. And, of course, we've been awaiting your advice."

"Yes, I understand. Well, I'm sorry you missed the action. And we're all sorry that we couldn't cover your bid. There was simply no way. Your, uh, competitor upstaged you. He sent it to Long Island."

"He did what?" was the surprised strongside response.

"He sent it to Long Island. Lot dump. Nineteen tons. In a meat truck."

Dead silence. After a moment, then: "That is very strong news. When was this?"

"About daybreak."

"A master stroke, would you say?"

"Oh, it caused quite a scramble in the pits, believe it. Your competitor may well be on his way to becoming an overnight folk hero. You know how the brokers love to gossip."

From the hardsite: "Well this is all very surprising. Our friend is looking stronger than anyone had suspected. Perhaps we made the cut too close. That makes it a clean sweep for his side, then. We sent out a twenty bid. We get one back, and nineteen are delivered to Long Island at daybreak. I wish we'd known this earlier, Peter."

"As I said, it has been a warm and busy time. With the heat and all, you know, it's sometimes very difficult to do precisely the right thing at precisely the right time."

"Oh sure, we understand."

"You say you got one back?"

"Yes. We got the kiss back. But rather badly used. We were forced to discard it. You can use a kiss but once, anyway."

"Uh, yes, that's true. Are you sure it bounced back clean?"

"That's why the internal cool, Peter. Making sure. It seems to be okay. I wish we'd known about the other. This is going to call for an entirely new sales program. Have you any advice?"

"Not at this time, not really. In a couple of hours, maybe. Meanwhile, a party of buyers is headed your way. Look for them any time within the next hour or so. At the airport."

"I see."

"Yes."

"Well. Okay. It is a rather large delegation?"

"Large enough, yes. But you could supply them, I believe."

"What is the exact purpose of the visit?"

"That has not been fully disclosed. It's a buying trip, though, believe it. It could alter your program considerably. I would suggest that you hold further bids until they settle the market."

"Oh. I see. Yes. Which marketplace are they from?"

"You know."

"Oh. Really? Okay. We'll be on the lookout. Peter—thank you so much for the market report. But, really, I wish we had known sooner. There could have been some small recovery possible. I regret that there was not."

"So do I, Simon. So do I. Well ... watch out for local heroes. They can become very tiresome."

"They also can be undone by heroic excesses, Peter. Has it started?"

"Oh yes, it has certainly started. That's what I meant by holding your bids. Sorry, I thought you understood that."

"I understand it now. Thank you again, Peter."

A click and a hum signaled an end to the conversation. Five seconds later, the recorder shut down. Bolan removed the tape and put in a fresh one, then fed the recording to the computer for voice-print programming.

No dice. There was nothing the computer could tell him about those voices.

There was quite a bit that Bolan could tell himself, though. Both of those guys were headshed Aces. He would bet his life on it. And the game was getting very tricky.

He reflected briefly on his recent experiences in Atlanta, trying to find a logic in the overall weave which would explain Pittsfield in more than the catch-all generality of *purge*.

They were purging, sure—but nothing seemed to fit the way it should. While in Atlanta, Bolan had decided that it was some sort of factional power play—the age-old game of dominance among savages, territorial disputes which were now in the early stages of move and countermove, and which ultimately would erupt into a red-hot war. It was all very disturbing, and not because Bolan gave half a damn if they all just wiped one another out—but the game never seemed to end that way. Usually it ended with one or more factions sealed more firmly than ever before at the table of infinite power.

The only reason that the mob had not succeeded in completely devouring the world until now was because of that inner balance—that competition between the savages which kept them all in various positions of restraint.

If those guys ever did succeed in becoming *completely* mobbed up, then there would be no stopping them anywhere. They would indeed rape the world and eat it, too.

Bolan had to find out what was happening in Pittsfield, who was making it happen, why. And not just because of Leo. Because of the entire gentle world. It could not survive the truly dominant savage.

He went outside and disconnected the tow vehicle and began laying plans for another scouting expedition. If he'd interpreted that guarded conversation between the Aces correctly, a large head party was coming in by air. Bolan wanted to be on hand to check them in and take their number.

It seemed that others shared that thought with him. When he went back inside the warwagon, the audio monitors were quivering with the ghostly echoes of automobile engines firing up and voices raised in excited exchanges. The video recorders clicked on a moment later. Bolan went to that monitor for a look.

And, yeah, a caravan was forming down there. He counted five cars through the gate, then put the warwagon in motion and began a casual descent to the state road.

So okay. They'd *all* go to the airport to welcome the new "buyers."

Bolan's old home town was rapidly becoming a seller's market.

It was a "company plane," yeah—a big jet which many smaller airlines would have been proud to call their own. It touched the runway with hardly a quiver and rolled smoothly into the deceleration. Bolan's VHF radio monitors were turned to the local control channels. He had overheard the landing and taxi instructions and knew the precise spot where the big craft would be unloading her passengers. Even that fit the usual pattern. They would not debark through the regular terminal, but would unload at the base operator's hangars.

The warwagon was a quarter-mile removed from that scene. Bolan was on high ground with unrestricted visibility, looking straight down the barrel with the entire airport complex in full side profile to his optic systems. If it had been his desire, Bolan could have read the headlines of a newspaper lying on the ground at either side of the terminal.

Except for a bit of movement in the base operator's area, the whole place lay serenely inactive. A small single-engine plane was making touch-and-go practice landings on the main runway, yielding briefly to the arrival of the big jet, then resuming its monotonous circling in the airport traffic pattern. A service vehicle was parked in the grass near the end of the runway, while a maintenance man checked the lighting system.

Out front, two cars and a pickup truck were the only occupants of the terminal parking lot. The five big cars from Club Taconic were pulled into a semicircular drive in the base operator's hangar area. They had been there when Bolan arrived, unoccupied except for their wheelmen, who sat tensely at their stations and chainsmoked throughout the long wait.

That was a disturbing note, which Bolan had recognized the moment he made the scene.

Disturbing, because each of those vehicles had left the hardsite fully loaded. They were obviously not here to provide transportation for the arriving delegation—yet that was exactly the image being presented.

But where were the hardmen?

Bolan had been searching for signs of them for a full twenty minutes. Twice he had caught flickers of movement in the interior of the big hangar building and once he'd picked up a ghostly refraction from a service window at the office—an image of several men in coats and ties hurrying past.

A guy in mechanic's coveralls seemed to be spending a lot of time doing nothing to a Piper Comanche in the tiedown area.

Another guy sat with an open magazine in the cab of a fuel truck parked on the service apron. Strangely, he never seemed to turn a page, and he was not really looking at the magazine most of the time.

It was a set, sure.

Super security, maybe—a courtesy to the visitors to insure their safe arrival in the city—but then again, maybe something else entirely.

Bolan had kept that scene under close surveillance throughout the wait, and now that the plane had touched down he was giving it particular attention. There was a lot of movement down there, now, though furtive and hardly noticeable even under the big eye of the warwagon. Then came the clincher. As the plane taxied to a halt, three guys stepped out of a side door at the far end of the hangar, dull blue gunmetal gleaming momentarily in the sunlight before the three disappeared once again behind a stack of crated machinery. A glimpse was all it took. Those guys had automatic weapons.

And it was a full set, yeah. Someone did not appreciate the competition in this seller's market and they had moved swiftly and decisively to protect the territory.

Ordinarily Bolan would have sat back and

watched and counted the dead, perfectly content to let the enemy engage itself. This time, it was different. He would prefer to see a natural balance of power in this arena—at least for awhile, until the various pieces could be sorted out and classified.

He had thought ahead to this moment, from that first uneasy suspicion of things awry. Now, he knew exactly how he wished to play the situation.

He punched the "Fire Enable" control on the command console and awaited the green light which would signal that the roof-mounted launchers were raised and locked. The sequence was perfect; he had a "Fire Enable Go" within ten seconds, and "Target Acquisition Positive" within fifteen.

A target grid with rangemarks became superimposed upon the optics monitor and the little red diode began its frantic flashing.

The choice of target was, of course, highly important. The Executioner did not make war on helpless civilians and innocent bystanders. He could not know how many gentle lives were caught up in that target zone, so he could not target indiscriminately. There was going to be gunplay, regardless. Innocents were going to suffer even if Bolan did nothing whatever.

And, yeah, he had his targets. It was not a kill mission, but a calculated save.

He set acquisition for automatic double and delineated the desired tracks, then balled his fist and punched his knee.

*One away!*

He punched his knee again immediately, and the second rocket rustled away, a flaming arrow streaking unerringly along the target path in an awesome rush of doom!

Down below, at target central, two trumpeting explosions hardly a second apart sent fireballs lifting skyward and brought a new brightness to the day.

*Technology, yeah.*

In the final analysis, Mack Bolan knew that all were savages and all was savagery—technology included.

The only question to be answered by the technicians was, simply, who was to be the greatest savage of all.

For as long as he could take the fire to the others, Mack Bolan was determined that he would be.

# CHAPTER NINE

## The Fire

Billy Gino was the first man through the door. He stood there for a moment at the top of the steps, surveying the scene, then moved aside and sent a couple of boys down to the ground. "Check it out," he growled. "See if the cars are ready. Give me a beep when it's clear."

The boys went on down and hurried across to the hangar—a distance of about 100 feet. He watched them inside, then sent another pair down with instructions to cover the debarkation from the tail of the plane. Another pair descended to cover the forward area.

David called out to him from the interior: "How does it look, Billy?"

He stuck his head inside for a moment to reply, "Looks pretty clean, sir. Almost deserted. Line of cars over by the hangar—should be ours. It'll be just a minute or so."

He was just in the process of returning his attention to the outside situation when something very remarkable happened over there in that "line of cars."

Billy had but a flashing impression of some object streaking across the terminal area and impacting in the midst of those cars. He was nearly thrown to the ground by the concussive force as a fireball whoofed skyward and one of those vehicles disintegrated right before his eyes—and he was still trying to save himself from a fall when another streaker rustled across for a quick encore.

As the second vehicle went to hell the instant way, Billy flung himself flat atop the boarding platform and screamed the unnecessary warning: *"Everybody down!—get down!—it's an ambush!"*

A furious fusillade from several choppers unloading in concert tore out of the open hangar to spray the big plane at window level from head to tail. Continuous muzzle flashes from the side of the hangar ripped the flight deck and demolished all the glass up there. His four boys on the ground were all down and only the angle of fire coming up that steel ladder was saving Billy Gino from an identical fate.

He had his .45 in his paw and roaring back defiantly before he was even consciously aware that he had responded. Someone had run forward to the flight deck and was shooting through the shattered windows. He heard David yelling for people to get up and return the fire. Pistols began crackling from several smashed windows along the cabin line.

He could see people moving about inside that hangar, now, and there seemed to be some confusion in that sector.

Some guy over there yelled, *"It's a suck! We've got fire behind us! That's our cars burning back there!"*

So much had happened in so short a time. It could not have lasted for more than a few seconds. Debris was still settling from those blasts in the vehicle area. Besides the two cars which had been blown away, two more were ablaze and a fifth was smoking and blistering from the intense heat.

But that was not the end of it.

Almost as if to punctuate the worried shout from the hangar, another of those whizzers came streaking in and hit the fuel truck.

Billy Gino momentarily blacked out. He felt rather than heard the explosion and had an instant visual perception of the awesome firestorm radiating away from the strike; the next awareness was of shit flying through the air everywhere, and of so much heat that he thought his flesh was afire. He was still lying atop the boarding platform. The shooting had stopped completely.

He dragged himself inside the plane and lay there sucking air like a fish out of water.

David was on his hands and knees, staring at him with a shocked look in his eyes.

"For God's sake, what is it?" Eritrea asked his bodycock.

Billy Gino did not even attempt to reply to that. The answer was too obvious.

What it was, David boy, was doomsday. And the heat from hell had already arrived.

# CHAPTER TEN

## Shockwaves

The survivors were huddled in blankets in the main terminal building, a thoroughly subdued and thankful bunch if Billy Gino had ever seen it.

Cops were all over the place, of course—and they'd reconstructed most of it to their apparent satisfaction. The really surprising thing was that they did not seem to be throwing any weight against the Long Island visitors. In fact, they were giving them the same courtesies and consideration as the other "victims"—the airport employees who'd been seized and bound by the "gunmen" when they had taken the place over.

The big guy in plain clothes had identified himself as a Captain Weatherbee. He was a homicide dick. The other one was a detective sergeant named Pappas. Neither had said a hell of a lot, although it was pretty obvious what they were thinking. They'd given no more than a passing squint at Billy's credentials and gun permit. Really, the guys were being pretty decent about the whole thing. Maybe the whole scene was just too much for a town the size of Pittsfield to handle—or to even want to handle. Although certainly they seemed to be taking care of the "disaster" with admirable efficiency. Paramedics were all over the place, tending to minor hurts, and the ambulances were screaming back and forth in a steady stream. And you sure couldn't fault those guys in the fire department, the way they'd come in there and ...

Billy Gino shivered.

Most of the stuff in those ambulances was going to be DOA. Billy was still trying to figure out why his own mortal clay was not among them. His whole face was singed. He did not have an eyelash left and he probably would not need to shave for a week. Yet, he'd suffered more pain from summer sunburns, as a kid.

David had a small cut under his left eye—from flying glass, probably—but that was about the extent of his injuries.

It was a damn miracle.

And, sure, Billy Gino was counting his blessings.

He'd lost about a dozen boys. Also the flight crew. Also the company plane, although it could maybe be salvaged if they could ever get it dug out of the the damn foam. He had six walking wounded and two more on stretchers who had at least a fifty-fifty chance. The rest of those bodies—in roasted bits and pieces, mostly—belonged to someone else. Billy would not even attempt to estimate their number. Maybe another dozen, maybe more.

But Billy Gino had been hurt enough, yeah. Half his force was gone. And the others were plenty demoralized.

The cop, Pappas, had something in his craw he just could not seem to get rid of. Kept strolling around the place double-checking the eyewitness stories and muttering to himself. And Billy Gino had overheard the guy talking to his captain about the "containment."

"There's no flow over," the cop muttered. "We

have only one injured bystander, and he did it to himself leaping through the office window. All these other people are pedigree unknown."

Pedigree unknown, yeah—the guy had it all, right there. Billy Gino would have given a lot to learn some of those pedigrees. That little shit of a Leo Turrin had evidently imported himself some real hotshots. If the Pittsfield cops didn't know the guys, in a town this size, then . . .

And yet . . .

Billy leaned toward his boss and whispered, "Something stinks here. I believe we met *two* forces out there. I heard a guy yelling from the hangar just before it all went to hell. He was as surprised by those explosions as I was."

David's eyes still held a haunted look. He replied, "Those explosions saved our asses, Billy. You think about that. Think about where we'd be right now if it hadn't all gone to hell just when it did. They had us, Billy. They really had us wrapped."

And it was true, of course.

The big guy, Weatherbee, came over with a full bottle of Schenley's in a paper sack. He handed it over to David as he told him, "Compliments of the city health department. Enjoy. We won't detain you here any longer. But please go straight to your hotel and don't leave the city without getting in touch with me. Can I count on you for that?"

David graciously accepted the bottle and assured the big cop that he could be counted on to behave responsibly.

The guy gave him a nice smile and said, "Fine. Your transportation is right outside."

Boy, it sure wasn't New York City.

And it was all a bit puzzling. The guy wasn't that dumb. He knew what this "business party"

83

really was. He knew what had really happened out there on that airport service ramp. But there had not been a single embarrassing question.

Billy Gino had to wonder: did Leo have things nailed down *that* tight in Pittsfield?

A thought quivered in his mind as the survivors straggled outside for the ride into town. He plucked delicately at David's tattered coatsleeve and told him, "You know something—this is all kind of weird. This town acts like it's wired. I wonder who's holding the wires?"

"Whose town is it, Billy?" David asked softly.

That was it, yeah. It was Leo Turrin's town. That much must be very obvious, now, to anybody with hungry eyes for this most improbable territory.

"Then there's no doubt about it, is there," he told his boss. "It was Leo who saved us."

"You're probably right," David replied tiredly. He slid into the car beside his bodycock and added, very quietly, "That's not really the question, Billy. The question is this: Who was trying to *have* us."

That was the question, yeah, for damn sure.

And Billy Gino meant to have an answer to it before the day was totaled up.


To be sure, Al Weatherbee knew precisely what had happened there that day. Indeed, he'd been expecting some such fireworks for hours.

Brognola had called him from Washington in the middle of the night and dropped it on him straight from the blue.

"Mack Bolan is back, Al."

"Back where?" Weatherbee asked, still half asleep.

84

"Back where he started," was the awakening statement.

"Aw, shit!" Weatherbee muttered and reached for the bed lamp.

Alice was wide awake and looking at him. "What is it?" she asked, knowing probably from the look on his face that it couldn't be good.

"Put on some coffee, huh," he whispered to her, then cocked an ear to the open window and told the man in Washington. "You must be mistaken. I don't hear a thing."

"That's the idea and that's why I'm calling," Brognola replied. "I have a favor to ask, old buddy."

"If it's about that guy, forget the old buddy routine. I gave Bolan his chance a long time ago, and he told me what to do with it. For old times sake, sorry—but that's the way it is and that's the way it stays. You sponsor the guy if you think you must, but dammit don't ask—"

"Hey, hey, what kind of talk is that at four o'clock in the morning! You know damn well the guy told me the same thing he told you. There's no sponsorship—and I'm not asking you to do a thing on his behalf. Al, I've got a real difficult problem. My man there is in extreme jeopardy."

"Your man here is always in extreme jeopardy. He's lucky he escaped Bolan the first time around. I don't see how—"

"No, wait, please—let me tell it, huh? From go?"

Weatherbee sighed and reached for a cigarette. "So tell it," he growled.

"My man is caught in the middle of a gangland squeeze. We don't know, really, who is after him or why—but we do know that they've already ordered his coffin. I've got to go before the Senate this afternoon and—wait, no, let's skip all that. The point is, we believe the cover is intact and we'd like to keep it that way for bigger things to come. Okay, there's the picture. Now, enter Mack Bolan. A lot has happened since the guy left Pittsfield, Al—you know all about that. And there's a very special friendship—and, I might add, a highly beneficial friendship for us—between Bolan and my man there in Pittsfield. Okay. Now Bolan is aware of what is going down. He is in town right now on a save. That's all it is. He's not there to bust the town again. He's just trying to save it for the man."

"Little damn consolation there," Weatherbee sniffed. "When that guy moves, shock waves flow out all around him. I don't want him here, Hal. Take your man out and tell Bolan to leave with him."

"It isn't that simple. The man wants to stay. A lot of years have gone into this operation—you know that. You've always helped us in the past. I'm counting on that help again. Now, dammit, you tell me nay."

"Nay," Weatherbee said glumly, then swung his feet to the floor with a sigh and took it back. "Okay. How far does my neck stretch this time?"

"Not far. We are simply asking that you give Bolan some room and allow him to operate quietly. You know what I mean. Put your town on hard, sure—but handle it like any other rumble. Let's not have any screaming headlines about Mack Bolan coming home to do it again. There cannot be the merest hint of a collaboration between my man and Bolan. There's the whole game, see. Bolan isn't autographing a thing, and we are just asking that nobody do it for him. Otherwise my man will be in double jeopardy."

Weatherbee sighed and said, "Okay, I getcha. I'll try to play, Hal—but no promises. I don't have your autonomy, you know. I have to answer to—"

"*What* autonomy!" Brognola snorted. "I've got the whole damn U.S. Senate sitting on my ass at this very minute!"

"Good for you," Weatherbee said pleasantly and hung it up.

He'd gone then into the kitchen and told Alice. He always told Alice. Everything. He involved her in all his conspiracies of justice—because she worried less, that way—and because she'd promised for better or for worse.

"I'm on his side," was all Alice had to say about the new problem in town.

She'd said it before, of course, speaking of Mack Bolan. She romanticized the guy, as most women tended to do.

There were those moments when the big tough homicide cop would secretly admit to himself that he did the same damn thing.

"There's something about the guy you just naturally have to admire," he told his wife, over coffee in the kitchen that morning.

That was not how he put it to his chief later that morning, however, when he went to work.

"We have a federal sensitive request," he told the chief. "I don't like it and I don't expect you to like it, either. A brother officer's life is at stake, though, and I recommend we give it a go. A limited go, anyway—at least until we can see some very compelling reason not to do so." And he told the story just the way it had come to him. And, no, the chief did not like it a damned bit—but he did finally agree to a limited go.

And now, dammit, just look at the *unlimited gone!*

Bodies piled up in the morgue!

Hospital emergency overflowing with butchered flesh!

An appalling disaster scene at the airport!

The town crawling with imported hitmen and high-powered big city bosses!

Autographed or not, this amazing crap had the Bolan print all over it. Where the hell did that goddamn Brognola get off, saying "give the guy some room to operate."

Even Johnny Pappas, a Bolan fan from the very beginning, was finding it hard to assimilate. He watched the bewildered and bedraggled hoods slink away toward the comforts of the best hotel in town, then turned to his captain with a wink and a sigh.

"I haven't seen anything like this since Bolan went against old Sergio," he said quietly.

"You've guessed it," Weatherbee replied sourly.

"What guess?" the sergeant said. "The guy is back. His marks are all over it. I've double-checked all the eyewitness reports. The gun battle didn't last fifteen seconds. Like pushing a switch, it went on and it went back off again. Yet five automobiles and a gasoline truck were completely demolished, a big jet plane is sitting in ruins, and something like twenty-five men are dead. The count could go higher once we've sifted through all the rubble. But here's the clincher. All the dead and wounded are gunmen. The only property that was destroyed belonged to the combatants—except the gas truck, and it was that hit that brought the gun battle to a premature and screeching halt. How many lives were saved—and I mean possibly how many *inno-*

88

*cent* lives—when that gas truck went up? With all this hell breaking loose upon a public place, what sort of fantastic stage management did it take to keep the action confined to just those people and just that property?" The sergeant was arguing with himself. "Naw. Naw. Don't talk coincidence or luck to me. It's the Bolan touch. It's all over the thing."

"You're reading it as an ambush, then," Weather-bee said, just for the sake of discussion. He'd already come to the same conclusion, himself. "One gang came in here and took over the airport, seized and bound all the employees of the flying service, and waited for that plane to land. Someone else, a third party, was standing by and watching the play. He preempted the showdown with one of his own. He had a bazooka or some equivalent, and he just stepped in and took over. He confined his fire to the safe zones, and served it up primarily to alert the gang on the plane as to what they were walking into. Is that what you're saying?"

"Just about, yeah," Pappas replied, almost defensively, as though half expecting the captain to utterly destroy the logic with his next words.

"I think you're exactly right," Weatherbee said.

"You do?"

"I do. And I'd like to suggest, youngster, that you have not seen a damn thing yet."

Pappas gave him a slow, solemn smile and said, "Then you agree all the way? You're saying that Mack is back?"

"Oh, he's back, he's back," the captain said with a sigh.

Could anyone doubt it?

# CHAPTER ELEVEN

## Confirming It

If there had been any official doubts concerning the authorship of that stunning airport hit, they were soon to be dispelled. Weatherbee and Pappas were outside with the lab men, grimly examining the physical evidence, when a uniformed cop came looking for them. He had a teenager in tow. "This young man has a story you'll want to hear, Captain."

Weatherbee turned tiredly to the boy and said, "I'm listening."

The kid was fairly bursting with the report—eyes dancing excitedly, breath staggering. "I'm a student pilot. I was practicing touch and goes. I was up there when everything started. I was on the downwind and I saw this missile or rocket. It came out of about one four five, flying low and moving like hell. Then, *whizzz*, another one—right on the first ones' tail.

"I couldn't see the hits because it was over my shoulder in the blind. But I banked up and saw the fireballs rising up like an atomic attack. No kidding, just like in the movies. That was my first thought—oh God no, it couldn't be. I nearly lost the stick, I was so shook up. I pulled out and started climbing into the upwind. Guess I lost my head for a minute. I broke the pattern completely.

91

Then I was coming back around to pick up the pattern. The tower was yelling at me to clear the zone. I was jockeying around up there when the third one let loose—and this time I saw the whole thing. It came off that knoll down there across from Johnson's. All of a sudden it just flashed up and there it was, hissing along at about treetop level, I guess. I thought at first it was going right for the tower, but I had a bad angle on it. Boy those things really travel! It whizzed on behind the tower and smacked into the gas truck—*flammm*—I mean I had a ringside seat and I saw the whole thing. It hit right on the side of the fuel tank. I could see the exact point where it hit, and the initial flash—and then, wow, what a sight! I was close enough that the shock wave bounced me around and I almost lost control again. When I got stabilized and looked again, everything down here was obscured by flames and smoke."

Weatherbee had been watching the boy closely throughout that breathless recital. He said quietly, "That's an amazingly well put together report, son. It almost sounds like you've been rehearsing it."

The kid's eyes crackled at that insinuation. He said, "I've told it about ten times. I guess you could call that rehearsing. I told it like it was. Exactly."

"Okay, I apologize," Weatherbee said solemnly. "The area was covered with smoke and flames. Go on. What did you do then?"

"The tower sent me out to a holding pattern until the emergency could be cleared. I had plenty of fuel so it was no sweat. I got back down just a little while ago—and I ran for a cop."

Weatherbee smiled and said, "Good for you."

"That throws our bazooka theory to hell," Pappas commented.

Weatherbee still had eyes for the kid. He asked him, "You say you saw the third missile all the way, and that it came from way down by Johnson's—the hamburger joint? That's nearly half a mile away, isn't it."

The kid was not intimidated by the policeman's stare, nor was he to be misled. "About fifteen hundred feet sir, on a course of three one zero from the end of the runway. I use it as a marker. The missile flashed up off that knoll to the west."

"Could you pinpoint the actual launching site?"

"Yes, sir, I think I could. I know I could from the air. I fly over that area about fifty times a week."

"You didn't see the launcher itself?"

"Well it just sort of flashed out of the trees up there."

"Out of the trees," Weatherbee murmured.

"Yes, sir."

Pappas let out a loud sigh.

Weatherbee gave the kid a friendly smile and told him, "I appreciate it. Go back inside and have a coke or something, but don't go away, eh. I'll want you to take us up there in a few minutes. Okay?"

The kid beamed back at him and said, "Sure. I'll be glad to. I can't fly you, though, I'm still on—"

"You bet you can't," Weatherbee said, grinning. "We'll have a look at ground level."

The youngster returned to the terminal. Weatherbee looked at his sergeant and said, "There you go. Flashed up out of the trees, the man said. Now you tell me what the guy was using."

"Sure wasn't any bazooka I've ever seen," Pappas

agreed. He sighed again. "You know, I've been following the guy pretty closely ever since he left town. I mean, I have a pretty thorough file on his activities. You'd think the guy would be rather well frazzled out by now, wouldn't you. But no. He gets better and stronger all the time. There have been some rumors . . ."

"Go on," Weatherbee demanded.

"Well it's never been confirmed, but there has been some official conjecture that the guy has got himself some sort of tank."

"Some sort of what?"

"Not exactly a *tank*—not a military—some kind of vehicle with some pretty crazy firepower. Now these men up here in the tower didn't see anything until just before the moment of impact. They both agreed, though, that it was some sort of missile. As opposed to artillery, or anything that could be thrown by hand. The physical evidence confirms it. Whatever came slamming into here was damned powerful, and it had armor-piercing capability. Now the kid is telling us that it came from a quarter of a mile away. With pinpoint accuracy, yet. Let's go look at that site, Cap."

"Let's do that," Weatherbee agreed heavily.

By all means.

And if that damn guy had himself a tank, indeed, then he'd already used up all the "limited go" he was going to get in *this* town.

"You put a good strong watch on our friends from Long Island, didn't you?" Weatherbee grumped.

"Yes, sir—we've got a four-unit surveillance on them."

"You'd better put on four more," the Captain

94

said soberly. "I have a feeling this town hasn't seen anything, yet."

It was more than a feeling, though.

It was a screaming certainty.

Mack the Ripper was home again.

# CHAPTER TWELVE

## And Getting Warmer

Bolan had abandoned the firing line immediately after getting strike confirmation, then moved swiftly to a surveillance station at the airport approach. He watched the disorganized withdrawal of the bunch from the hardsite, grimly numbering their remains and taking note of the mental atmosphere there. And, no, it was not a retreat, but the rout of a decimated and demoralized force. They had arrived in five vehicles; they departed in two hastily appropriated from the rental lot behind the flying service building.

Bolan dismissed them and let them run; he knew where to find them when he wanted them. The chief interest now was with the other force—and they too had suffered grievously. Bolan was there, watching, throughout the emergency response by city and county—and he was there, still watching, when the last of the survivors took their humiliating departure. Yes, they had suffered. Hardly thirty guns were left—and there were some surprising faces in that collection.

He followed that procession to its destination—a downtown hotel—and cruised slowly past as the battered men gathered themselves on the sidewalk outside.

He would know where to find these, also. He left

them there to nurse bruised egos and hurting flesh, proceeding on through the city to stop at a public telephone on the outskirts.

He connected with Leo Turrin's clean line on the first try and told him, "Okay, it's off and running."

"So I see," said the underboss of Pittsfield. There was a wry twist to his words. "I've been watching you on TV."

"Did I look pretty?"

"Positively beautiful. You're a hell of a guy! Don't you even *care*? I spotted your damn bus, buddy, right down there in the thick of it. What a hell of a nerve!"

"What's the official call, Leo?"

"There isn't one, yet. I saw your old friend Weatherbee, too, but it was just a quick glimpse. They were shoving TV microphones at him and trying to pry a statement loose. No way. That guy is as cool as they come. So the news people were left with their own assumptions. They're hypothesizing everything from an aborted hijack to a terrorist attack." The fed chuckled nervously. "One guy even said that it was painfully reminiscent of the days when Sergeant Mack Bolan was stalking the town."

Bolan commented, "A lot of people are going to be reaching that conclusion, Leo. I guess the quiet game is over. I hated to blow it away this soon but I just had to step in there. I think maybe a saving grace has come to town and I couldn't allow it to disappear in an airport ambush."

"Did you say a saving grace?"

"Uh huh. Didn't you see anyone else you know on TV today, Leo?"

"No. Nobody surprising."

"Would you have been surprised to see David Eritrea—or Billy Gino—or Rocky Tamiano?"

"Were they there?"

"They were. You'll find them right now at the regular watering hole. They managed to squeeze through about thirty guns. I guess Weatherbee decided to cool them on through. He's got them staked out like fresh meat, I'd guess, just waiting for another nibble."

"Well, wait. This can get very confusing. Which—?"

"We have second and third parties making war on your turf, Leo. I agree that it is confusing. Eritrea was bringing a war party into town when he was jumped by the other one. The other one is very clearly tied directly into your problems, already. I don't know where the hell Eritrea fits but—"

"He's Augie's *consigliere*."

"So he is. So since when does a *consigliere* lead a war party?"

"Well, Billy Gino is the man for that role. Eritrea must be standing in for Augie. So that means . . ."

"Right," Bolan solemnly agreed. "Who's pushing the purge?"

"I guess it isn't Augie," Turrin quietly decided.

"What made you think so in the first place?" Bolan wondered.

"I don't know, it just fell in that way. Number One, he's sponsoring me. Nobody with a right mind would come after me without Augie's clear consent. Number Two, I tried for days to talk to him and nobody would put me through. That is tracks enough on the wall for anyone, buddy. So if it's not Augie . . ."

"The local push is coming straight out of the *Commissione*, Leo."

"What?"

"Yeah. There's an Ace in this hardsite in the north hills who is currently calling himself Simon. His contact in New York is using Peter as a handle. That's sort of biblical, isn't it—Simon, Peter. I tangled with an Ace Trio down in Atlanta a couple of days ago who were calling themselves John, Paul, and James."

"That's very interesting," Turrin murmured.

"It sure is. I've been sort of wondering . . . who's calling himself Jesus?"

Turrin made a sound with his lips and said, "Listen, Sarge, this sounds like big stuff."

"You're reading along with me, then."

"What else to read? Someone is trying to engineer a complete takeover. And they've bought themselves a house of Aces to stack the game."

Bolan asked, "When was the last time you talked to Augie?"

"Couple of weeks ago. I usually try to check in with him a couple of times every month. Everything has been beautiful, until a few days ago. Suddenly I'm a leper."

"Maybe it just fell in that way. Maybe it's a false reading. Maybe there's another explanation for Augie. How's his health?"

"Not exactly roses, since Jersey. But he's been the *boss*, no mistake about that. He sounded okay to me two weeks ago."

"What if he's not okay now, Leo? Suppose the old man is on his death bed right now? And suppose the word got out to some ambitious young Turks. How would you read a play like that?"

"Just about like this one," Turrin replied quietly.

100

"How's your relations with Eritrea?"

"Good enough. A bit of jealousy there, maybe. Other than that . . ."

Bolan said, "Okay, I think you may be hearing from him. I think maybe he came to town to find out just what the hell is going down here. He got your message out on Long Island this morning. Now he's come to find out what it means. So make yourself available for a call. But don't commit your life to that guy's hands, Leo. Let's play him very carefully."

"Oh, sure."

"Another thing. It's liable to get very rough around here before it all blows off. I can't believe that anyone hooked into the *Commissione* would risk a shooting war over turf like this. No disrespect meant—you know it better than anyone. There's nothing here worth the effort being expended. So all this has to have another meaning. We need to know, Leo, why Pittsfield fell heir to the war."

"There's nothing to say it was ever planned that way."

"No, there is not. And probably it was not. But someone is guilty of a miscalculation, at the very least. They're not just blundering around dumb and blind. I could have bought some of that from the Boston and Albany boys—but not from the headshed."

"Yeah. Okay. I go along with that. Don't overlook your part in the thing, though, Sarge. It started off as an easy push, not a war. The war came when you came. Remember that."

Bolan said, "Uh huh. Okay. Just play it close, Leo. And listen—they're probably already starting

101

to wonder. If Eritrea contacts you, I want you to finger me."

"What?"

"You're the Bolan expert. Keep it covered. Tell Eritrea that you smell me. There's been time enough, now, for it to fit the logic. They knew I was in Atlanta and they know I left there two days ago. Natural progression, buddy."

"I see it, yeah, okay. And I'll cool it."

"Don't just cool it. Cover it with frost, buddy. Tuck it in and keep it down."

Turrin laughed. "How come you're so damn good at giving sensible advice to everyone but yourself?"

"I'm expendable," Bolan replied lightly.

"The hell you are," Turrin muttered.

"No tears on my grave, guy," Bolan mildly chastised his friend.

"Well you just keep one thing in mind," the little guy railed back. "A lot of people in this damn town are on my side. All I have to do is find the cut and make it. You can't do that, guy. You've got no cuts to make because you've got no friends to take. This whole damned town is waiting to eat you whole. So you watch it. You hear me, dammit? Watch it!"

"Thanks for caring, Leo. I'll do that."

"Me, too," the little guy said and abruptly hung it up.

Bolan went back to his battleship and headed for the hills.

Do that, yeah. Bolan would do that. He would watch the whole thing into a roaring conflagration.

And the town was already getting warmer with each hour that passed. Pretty soon, there would be a flash point.

And, sure, he would watch for that, too.

## CHAPTER THIRTEEN

## Kingdom Coming

Bolan resumed the vigil above the hardsite and settled in for a possibly tedious surveillance of the enemy's forward post of the new war zone. The movements down there were few and routine but there were vague evidences at about eleven o'clock of a general council in progress—a meeting of the full war party—perhaps a pep talk, perhaps something else entirely.

Everyone had gone inside except the gatemen— and it was not for chow, because Bolan had a rather clear view into the kitchen and the only activity there was beer service.

So it was a parley, sure, and Bolan was betting on a combat briefing. They had closed all the windows. The audio was picking up nothing. There had been no telephone activity since Bolan resumed the watch. The parley dragged on for an hour and a half.

Bolan used that time to refurbish his own war effort. He brought the launch elevator down and rearmed with a full pod, then raised it back into the roof and cycled the systems to standby. He also took the opportunity to haul out his personal combat rig and get it ready for another EVA.

After that, it was just wait and watch. His mind wandered along the problem, trying to fit pieces together and finding nothing particularly new or intriguing with which to finish the fit.

At one o'clock he turned a radio to one of the local broadcast stations and picked up on the news. Mack Bolan was back, yeah—that was the news story of the day in Pittsfield. Captain Weatherbee had released the official police view of the matter at the airport. Bolan took note and nodded appreciatively at the "captain" status. The first time around, Weatherbee had been a lieutenant.

There was very little actually reported on the day's activities. No mention whatever was made of the identities of the "airplane victims." Bolan tipped his mental hat to Weatherbee for that one, too.

The rest of it was a rehash of the past.

Bolan turned it off and went out to climb a pole.

If the news was out, then maybe it was time for another manipulation of a pressure point.

He patched in his handset and gave the guy a call.

"It's Bolan," he said, sort of whispering in the way he'd heard earlier. "Tell Simon, please."

"What's that again?"

"You heard it, buddy. Tell Simon."

He decided that the Aces were using some sort of masking device on the telephone mouthpiece. The guy came on just a bit uptight, but with that same whispery quality to the voice.

"This is Simon. What kind of dumb gag is this?"

Bolan replied in his natural voice—cold and hard. "No dumber than you want to make it, guy. What are you trying to pull? I closed this territory down a long time ago. Now you shag it the hell out of here."

A considerable silence followed. Bolan thought he heard another instrument join the connection

104

but he would not swear to that. When the guy finally replied, the tone was distant and formal. He said, "Then that really was you. This morning."

"It was me," Bolan assured him. "You shouldn't have exposed yourself that way. Now I've got you wired. I'm giving you ten minutes to break camp and take it away. And you take it west, not south. Clear out of the state, guy, and don't stop until you get to Albany."

Another overlong wait, then: "What's your interest?"

"Same as ever," Bolan told him. "I can't stand the stink of Mafia—especially not so close to the family plot. Move it, or I'll move it for you."

Simon seemed to be studiously avoiding any recognition of threat. He said, in that same formal stilt, "What about those other guys?"

"They're not camping out, guy. You are."

"That's how you found us, eh. You were on *them*. So now you're on us."

"That's where I am. Ten minutes. It's all I'll give."

"Where'd you get my name?"

"Same place I get everything else. That ten minutes is only a reprieve, Simon, not a pardon. I'll be getting around to you pretty quick, wherever you are. I was just down in Atlanta, you know."

"No, I didn't know that," the guy lied.

"James knew it. So did Paul. And so did John. The names are pretty cute. Which one of you guys is Judas?"

Another of those long silences enveloped the connection. When the guy came back, it was mad as hell. "Don't push us too hard, Bolan," he warned.

"I'll push it however and wherever I choose," the Executioner told the Ace. "Right now I'm pushing it

105

the hell off this territory. But you play it as dumb as you please."

The guy chuckled, but it was not an entirely convincing sound. He said, "You know, I'm really enjoying this. Tell you the truth, I can't believe it's happening. I've heard about the nutsy stunts you pull but I'd never believed it. Now I believe it. I'm scared to death, guy. Really. I'm shaking all over."

"Way to go," Bolan said, and broke the connection.

He returned to the warwagon and immediately activated the fire system. He had not been playing word games with the guy; he had been working toward a specific and calculated effect. Unless he was getting terribly stale at the game, he expected an immediate result.

And, yeah, he was getting it.

That yard down there was suddenly swarming with people. They were sending out walking patrols armed with choppers and beefing up the gate detail. A couple of guys appeared on the roof. He could hear shouted instructions on the audio pickup and he even picked up a couple of ghostly rumbles from inside the house. Then someone opened an upstairs window and began pacing back and forth in front of it.

Bolan zeroed the optics on that point and beamed in an infra-red supplement but the angle was bad and all he could get were shadowy figures. There were at least two people in that room, though, that much was certain—and they were having a very urgent parley. The barrel mike could get nothing better than isolated words, an occasional string of cusswords delivered with considerable emotion, a background rumble of angry voices during most of it.

But there was no doubt as to the reaction. He had struck a very live nerve with that telephone conversation.

The pacing figure at the upstairs window disappeared abruptly. A moment later, two guys came charging out through the front door and ran to a car—one of those used in the airport getaway.

Bolan enabled the rocketry and crosshaired that vehicle as it sped along the drive toward the gate. He tracked it into acquisition and gave it a couple of lengths on beyond the open gate, then he banged his knee and sent them a reminder of what was going down here in Pittsfield.

The rocket leapt away and found its firetrack instantly, veering into the target slot and rustling along in fiery intercept. The armor-piercing nose kissed the target three inches below the hood ornament and erupted into a thunderous wreath of fire that engulfed the vehicle and blew it all the way back to the gate.

The secondary from the gas tank erupted a heartbeat behind the hit to fling flaming droplets in a hellish shower clear back to the house, along with other debris that had been borne aloft by the double blast.

Battle-shocked people were running around down there and screaming at one another in unintelligible phrases when Bolan disabled the fire and tucked it back in. He went over to the audios and readjusted the sensitivity, then returned to the con and watched the reaction below.

There were no foolish soldiers down there. Not a head was showing anywhere. Everything was under cover. The gate was demolished and the earth around it cratered. An entire section of the fence was down. Still, nobody was showing.

It was a cautious force, and Bolan had to reflect on that. He reflected for about ten minutes while waiting for something to show. But nothing showed. The fire at the gate burnt itself out; otherwise the scene remained unchanged.

"Now you can shake, Simon," Bolan muttered tiredly, and he went out to climb the pole again.

He had a brief talk with Leo Turrin and learned that Eritrea had made contact. David had expressed his "amazement" over the distressing situation on Leo's turf, and promised his full support. The men from Long Island needed a few hours to get it back together; also, the local cops had them staked out and on short leashes. However, David would be getting back with Leo very shortly. Perhaps they could have dinner together.

Turrin had gracefully declined the dinner invitation, pointing out that his head was still being desired for someone's platter—but he promised to contact Eritrea before nightfall.

That was the way things stood in town.

Bolan did not go into the details, but he filled Leo in with regard to the developments in the countryside. And he added, "This is a super-cautious force, Leo. They are playing a very large game and they're playing it close to the chest. But I'm pushing their noses in the ground—and they won't take that for long. I look for a boilover very soon. So you keep it tucked in. I suggest you contact Brognola and try to find out where you stand in the Washington scene. And tell Hal what I said about the boilover. He should be on the alert for special pressure moves and try to follow the play from his end. And make sure all your ends are tucked in tight."

Leo assured his friend that he was thoroughly safed, and the conversation ended on that note.

When Bolan returned to the warwagon, a goody was awaiting him there. The telephone recorder had scored again. He quickly put the tape on the player and listened to the following conversation:

"Yes, hello."

The voice from the hardsite: "I had to risk the call, I'm sorry."

"Uh, just a moment." A chair creaked and a door closed in the background. Then: "Okay. I heard about your trouble."

"Why didn't you give us a call, then?"

"Too warm here, right now. I shouldn't be doing this, you know. Keep it brief. What can I do?"

"I don't know what you can do. You know the guy that hit the airport?"

"Yeah, we heard."

"Well I've got him."

A pause, then a surprised and delighted rejoinder: "You've *got* him! Well my God that's wonderful news!"

"Wait a minute, Peter."

"That's just what we've been needing. This is better than—listen, bring it on down here! Tell him I said that's exactly the sort of thing we've been needing. We'll arrange a triumphal entry. We'll ring the bells and pour the champagne and by God *dare* anybody to—"

The guy at the hardsite had been trying to break in through most of that delighted gabble. He finally succeeded with a shouted: "Peter, will you shut up and listen to me! You've got it wrong. I've got the guy, all right! But all over my bleeding back!"

That voice on the other end was now in deep chagrin. "*Coitus interruptus,*" it whispered bleakly.

109

"That's what that is, Simon. Hell I *knew* the guy was on your *back*. You shouldn't have—"

"Dammit he just hit me again!"

"Where!"

"Right here, dammit! And now I think we're under some kind of siege."

"Right *there*? How the hell did he—aw, dammit, Simon. That's the oldest damn—your boys led him right to it!"

"Maybe and maybe not. My boys aren't that stupid. Listen to this. The guy called me a couple minutes before this last hit. And—"

"What do you mean, called you? How did he call you?"

"On this damn telephone, Peter. He did not stand out in the damn yard and yell at me!"

"Simmer down. We're getting too worked up over this."

"*You* simmer down. I'm the one under the heat. Listen to what I have to say, then you tell me again to simmer down. He called my name. I mean my *name*. And he's got it tied, somehow. He also mentioned John, Paul, and James. Now you tell me where the hell he gets all that—and then I'll simmer down."

"He must have got it in Atlanta," Peter replied quietly. "I wonder how much he really got?"

"He didn't leave much in Atlanta, Peter."

"No, he did not."

"Well he's starting it here, now. And he's starting with me. I want some support."

"Let's not get, uh, not overreact, Simon. What does *he* say?"

"*He* says to call *you*. He's depending on you, Peter."

"It's that bad?"

"Yes it is. The guy is sitting out here somewhere right now. He has some kind of goddamned mighty impressive fireworks. And he's right on my damned back. I can't move. I can't even show a head at a window. I don't know where the hell he is and I'm not sending any boys out to look for him. I've lost half the force already. I'm not splitting up what's left in adventures with *that* guy in this kind of country. That would be playing his game, his way. So, now, we've got to have some support."

"Okay. I'll send you a battalion force. I can have them there in, say, four hours. Where do you want them?"

"I want them all over these damned hills. They should send me a signal when they get in place. Then we'll try to draw some fire. The rest is up to them. We picked a very bad spot here, Peter. It's practically indefensible from a guy like this."

"Nobody could have foreseen this situation, you know," replied the voice from the headshed. "Okay, don't worry, we'll recover it. You just sit tight and hold it."

"That's about all we can do, Peter. Don't let us down."

The conversation ended there. Bolan ran the tape through twice again, his mind picking at its pieces.

Who the hell was "*he*?" Someone on the hardsite, certainly. There had been no other calls recorded. Apparently those two guys who'd tried streaking out in the car had been on a message mission—and that must have been their only way.

So, yeah, *he* was on the site. Bolan recalled the impression that another telephone had been lifted into the connection shortly after the talk began—and he recalled also those long pauses occurring

111

during the conversation. They had been conferring offstage.

So okay.

Next—why were they so "indefensible?" They still had forty to fifty guns on board. If nothing else, they could simply blast their way clear and take their chances with the odds. Certainly any self-respecting army would not balk at that alternative against a single enemy—no matter how "impressive" the firepower.

So—it was as Bolan had already begun to suspect.

There was something at Pittsfield *to be defended;* not to be *taken* but to be *defended.*

So what the hell was it?

It was the territory nobody wanted. Wasn't it?

Obviously not!

Bolan had about four hours to find some answers. Which meant that he would have to push some noses a bit more firmly into the Pittsfield turf and hope to force the answers into the open.

From out of the gray matter, then, a possible answer popped loose and presented itself to the thinking mind.

Bolan sat back in the command chair and stared at his optic monitor.

Maybe he'd found "Jesus." Maybe "he" was "Jesus"!

And, for some very secret and highly important reason, maybe Pittsfield was to be the site of the throne for the new kingdom come to America.

Yeah. Oh, hell, yeah.

The fit was getting better all the time.

# CHAPTER FOURTEEN

## Boilover

The numbers in the game were becoming infinite.

When an Ace spoke of "batallion force" he meant exactly that. It included helicopters, spotter planes, special weapons and terrain vehicles—it was not a "war party" but an entire army numbering several hundreds of men.

Whatever the stakes on this turf, they were respectably high. Bolan knew that his time could now be measured in hours. It was no longer a waiting game. He had to get it done and get it out of there before the enemy response could take full form.

So he changed into special clothing and cycled his fire onto automatic standby. The fire control system was now meshed with the video surveillance. Anything which would activate the video would also enable the rocketry. Any sort of sustained movement in the target zone would then become an immediate target; the fire would launch itself and wait for another opportunity to speak.

Bolan had never used this particular capability of the fire systems, chiefly because he preferred to call his shots with more care and judgment than this "robot" could handle. The auto system could discern movements only, without distinction as to friend or foe. Any object of sufficient mass and velocity instantly became a target. Bolan did not like this choice of life and death conferred to a robot's electronic brain.

It was, however, an extraordinary time. And he had to use what he had.

He activated the base camp security system and went to town in the Ford. First on tap was a personal meet with Leo Turrin. He got the little guy on the phone and told him, "Okay, it's boiled over. We need an eyeball, right away. Where?"

Turrin quickly told him "where," and they met at a bowling alley, ten minutes later.

The undercover fed did not come alone. He was waiting in a car parked outside the meeting place—a wheelman and a tagman in the front seat, Leo and another guy in the rear. This was SOP, and entirely necessary. No ranking *mafioso* would venture into the unknown during such an unsettled time without the usual protections. Leo could do no less and still preserve the cover.

Bolan caught his eye and went inside. A ladies' league was in possession of all the lanes, and all were having a whale of a time. The only visible males in the place were a couple of employees working the desk.

Bolan stopped at the snack bar and bought a coke in a paper cup. He lit a cigarette and took the refreshment to a seat in the spectator's section, from which he watched the action in the lanes while Leo ran through his necessary routine.

Why, he wondered vaguely, did the ladies always seem to be having more fun than men doing the same thing? Less to prove, maybe, he decided—or maybe it was just an entirely different orientation to the life process.

Leo came in and took a seat in the next row be-

114

low. The two had the entire section to themselves and certainly nobody on the floor was giving them any attention. But "the life" had a way of making ruts in a guy's mind. Life and death habits were hard to break.

Leo simply sat there for about thirty seconds, apparently watching the bowling, before he turned in half-profile and casually commented, "There's some real tigers in here. How would you like to go against some of *those* babes?"

Bolan replied, just as casually, "Most of the tigers are outside, Leo. And I guess I'll be going against them in just a few hours, now, unless we can wrap this town."

"Sure. Hey, I had to make sure it was you, guy. Dammit, you're a regular chameleon. You look just like an Ace of Spades."

"That's the idea," Bolan muttered. He produced a small ID wallet and tossed it over.

Turrin took a look and tossed it back with a sigh. "Bingo," he said. "I'd buy it." He turned all the way to the rear and sent an eye signal to the little tagman who hovered quietly in the background. The guy gave Bolan a nervous dart of the eyes and retreated to the snack bar.

"Same guy," Bolan observed. "Fresni, isn't it? Don't you ever worry that he'll get wise?"

"Not Jocko," Turrin assured his friend. "He got his head squashed a little at the end of his last race. Never been much of a thinker, since. But he's the fastest gun in the East and the kind of loyalty he offers can't be bought anywhere. What's going down?"

Bolan succinctly told his friend what was going down, then added: "You can see the time problem.

We have to get it together, buddy. Are you cool with Eritrea?"

"Cool enough, yeah. Listen—it's still not too late to scratch this whole thing. I mean, it's getting—"

"No way, Leo. We've got to get you realigned. I'm reasonably certain that Eritrea is ripe for a talk. I don't believe he is your enemy—at least, not in this present thing. The guy didn't come all the way up here with a war party just to get the straight of a message dumped at his doorstep. Who is this guy you've been working at the *Commissione*?"

"His name is Flavia."

"Okay, that's the one. He came with Eritrea. He's here."

Turrin gave Bolan a shocked reaction. "Why do you think?"

"I don't know. But it almost has to bear on some sort of overlapping problem they've been having with the headshed boys. Listen, Leo—it's not inconceivable, is it—this entire thing may be centering around a *Commissione* revolt."

Turrin mulled that one for a moment before replying. "Okay," he mused aloud, "that's been one of the secret worries for years, of course. Those guys have too much power. There's a large area of operations where they are really autonomous. I mean, they answer to no one but themselves. The bosses are not the *Commissione*—not really. It's the body of government itself—what we call the bureaucracy, out here in the straight world. And, yeah, there is a lot of anonymous power afoot. That power reached its peak under the Talifero brothers—and I'll tell you something, buddy. Not everybody in the mob was real upset with you for putting those boys down. I mean, it was getting that bad."

"Maybe it's getting worse, under another Ace," Bolan said. "Which one would you suspect?"

"Hell, I don't even know those guys. A wink and a nod here and there, and that's about it. Nobody knows them, except the council of bosses themselves. And sometimes I think some of the bosses never really know who their Aces are. The guys change their names like flipping the sheets on a calendar—their faces, too. That's what makes it so damn creepy. You never really know who you're talking to in this organization. It gets really crazy, sometimes."

"Yeah," was Bolan's only comment to that. Yeah, for sure, though. He had been exploiting that particular facet of mob psychology for quite awhile and in many "crazy" places.

"So where does Flavia figure?" Turrin asked. "He's no Ace—he's just an office boy."

"I got the feeling while I was in Atlanta, Leo. Someone is really brokering power—and I've about decided that there are several factions at work. With Augie's firm hand off the tiller—hell, I don't know. It gets sort of crazy, like you said. Sounds okay when you're just thinking it. Putting it to words, it gets downright psychotic."

"I know what you mean," Turrin agreed. "Kick it around some, anyway. I've been psychotic for years."

Bolan chuckled. He lit another cigarette and took a quick scan of the background. Jocko Fresni was playing a pinball machine. Another guy stood near the door, making a prolonged study of the league schedules.

"Who's the guy at the door?" Bolan asked.

117

"My operations man, Joe Petrillo. Joe's okay."

"So let's talk psychotic. Augie is fading. The other bosses have been leaning against the old man for years. Who are they leaning on now? Which boss is strong enough to sit in Augie's chair?"

"None," Turrin replied immediately. "Augie is the last of the old street hellions. The other guys came into it by various other routes. There's not an Augie among them."

"Long live the king," Bolan said quietly.

"That's about it," Turrin agreed.

"So they'll cling to their king until there's nothing left to cling to. Where do they go then? To the king's man?"

Turrin considered that idea for a moment, then decided: "They could already be there. Eritrea has been sitting in Augie's council chair ever since Jersey. The old ones, okay—they might go with David. Guys like DiAnglia, Fortuna, Gustini. They hold the controlling interests, too. The other bosses ... I don't know. They come and go too fast to keep really up on." The little guy grinned. "A lot of attrition at the top. You wouldn't be knowing about that."

Bolan did not grin back. But, yes, he knew about that. The "attrition at the top" had been Bolan's chief preoccupation throughout the war. But it had begun to seem a futile task. The Mafia was a monster with infinite head-growing capability. Hack off one and another instantly appears to take its place.

He told Leo: "Maybe it's starting to pay. The attrition, I mean. Maybe that's what the current push is all about." He was remembering a whispery telephone conversation in the warwagon's recorder. "Maybe some one has decided that the leadership

118

is too mushy, that it's time to cut the deadwood and consolidate the base of power."

"I've heard that kind of talk," Turrin admitted. "Never very loud, though. Okay. Suppose it's true. Now what about Flavia?"

"Down in Atlanta, Leo, they were sitting on a tab that was nearly twenty years old."

"Whose tab?"

"That's the ironic part. There was no tab, really. It was something that had been hastily manufactured after a fizzled hit on Jake Pelotti. He was Saranghetti's underboss in Brooklyn and was about to be crowned Capo. Someone didn't like the idea and went after him. Are you with me?"

"That was before my time," Turrin replied musingly, "but I've heard talk about it. As you said, it fizzled. So now what?"

"So the police fished some bits and pieces out of the river a few days after that. It was identified as the remains of a guy with a small reputation as a free-lance hitman. It was suggested, at the time, that this was the guy who tried for Pelotti. You've heard the name John Paul James."

"Sure. You gave it to me awhile ago. The biblical bit."

"Right. Except there really was a John Paul James, and the name really belonged to a free-lance hitman. Now that's just too romantic to get past an imaginative Mafia mind, Leo. That name is central to this whole push, it's where the biblical code names got their start, and that twenty-year-old tab that wasn't a tab is, I think, the key to this whole bizarre thing."

"John Paul James did not make that hit?"

"Probably not, but that doesn't really matter.

The thing is that they went to Atlanta to collect a twenty-year-old tab."

"Uh, you left me somewhere. We were talking about Flavia."

"I still am. When you're brokering power, you look for tabs. Right?"

"Definitely. You go out and collect debts."

"Right. I was just making note of the fact that the collectors are out and that they are reaching very deep. I believe that David Eritrea could be playing the same game. He could figure that he has a tab on Flavia. And on you, Leo."

Turrin blinked at that. "Okay. Maybe he has. Flavia has been feeding me for three years. Part of my success with Augie is a direct result of that feed."

"So Eritrea may be here to call in the tab," Bolan said. "He's brokering you, Leo. So give it to him. Firm up the alignment. Make the cut and come down on it."

The little guy had a puzzled look. "It's where I've always been. Right with Augie. What's with tabs? The guy owns me body and soul already."

"You're speaking of Augie."

"Sure."

Bolan blew smoke toward the ceiling. "I'm speaking of David Eritrea."

Turrin's face settled into its normal lines. He chuckled. Then he told Bolan, "Maybe you're right."

"Let's give it a look, then. But cautiously, buddy. You know the game."

"Sure, I know the game. Don't worry. I'll work the guy to a fare-the-well."

"Okay. It's all I had, for now. One more thing, Leo. The hardsite is a joint out on the old Hancock Pike. It's called Club Taconic. Know the place?"

Turrin's eyes danced. "Sure, that's Manny Manila's old joint. He used to run a whore house out there, under Sergio. That was years ago. I phased that place down myself when I took over the girl operation."

"What's it like inside?"

"Well—it's been a few years. Big joint, as I recall. Lots of rooms upstairs—mostly small, but a couple of suites. Most of the downstairs was a big, open, party-room type of thing. Had a bar and a dance floor. Lots of plush furniture. A place for the girls to exhibit for the customer's choice."

"There are some smaller buildings off to one side," Bolan prodded.

"Oh, yeah. Bungalows. For special parties. You know."

Bolan knew. He said, "Who owns it now?"

Turrin spread his hands. "Manny sold out when he got the TB and went to Arizona. He died—couple of years ago, I guess. Had the siff, too, I think. Started going kind of crazy even before he went west. Who owns it now? I don't know. I sort of had the impression that the company took it off his hands. But I couldn't swear to that. The joint was too far out. I closed it up. Haven't been out that way since."

"Okay. We better break. I have a lot to do. So do you. Get with Eritrea. Set yourself a deal. Now's the time to drive a bargain, buddy. Make it a good one."

"Watch my smoke," the little guy said with a solemn smile. He was leaving his seat when Jocko Fresni came down to whisper something in his ear. Leo turned to Bolan and said, "Maybe you should wait here a minute. I got to return an urgent call. Came in on the car phone. Let's see what it is."

Bolan settled back and watched the ladies do their joyful stuff while Leo went to a phone booth near the snack bar.

The little guy was gone no more than a couple of minutes. When he returned, he looked like the very death. His face was gray and his eyes quivered as he slid tensely onto the seat next to Bolan.

"It's cut," Leo announced quietly.

"What's cut?"

"That was Hal. They've got my woman. They've got Angie."

Bolan's hackles stood tall as he growled, "*Who's* got her?"

"She's been snatched. Hal just found out a little while ago. But he says it looks like they came during the night. Lights were on all over the place and the bedside clock was pulled out of the wall at four-twenty-two. So that's all of it, buddy. I'm sorry, but that's all."

Bolan said, "Don't get crazy yet. Where was she stashed, Leo?"

"A safe house, on Cape Cod."

"A *government* safe house?"

"Yeah, but well covered. It seemed the best to do. Two of Hal's best men were there with her. Another one had gone on a campout with the kids—some CYO thing or something, on one of the islands. Hal said he just had so damn many things going in Washington he honestly didn't—oh, hell, Sarge, it's not Hal's fault. He tried to call there twice today and couldn't connect. And he had all these other things . . ."

The Bolan mouth was hard and grim as he asked his suffering friend, "How did he learn? Did someone make a contact?"

Leo shook his head. "No, they won't do it that way. They'll want me to sit and sweat awhile. They'll know that I'll know—the next move is up to me. I'll have to go down to the headshed, Sarge, you know—present myself. The right guy will find me."

"Give it awhile longer," Bolan urged. "Your life won't buy Angie a thing and you know it as well as I do."

"Hey, I can't think, I can't . . ."

Bolan had to talk the guy clear. "Are the kids okay?"

"Yeah, they're fine. Hal swooped them away under a full contingent—until the smoke clears, as he says. That's when they discovered the snatch, when the kids came back from the camparee. What the hell can I do, Sarge? I can't just sit here in the hole and—dammit, it's their game, now. I have to play."

"Get with Eritrea first," Bolan suggested. "Try to get an alignment firmed up, then see what you can work through the new channels. It's worth a try, Leo. And it could be Angie's only chance. You know how these guys play their games."

"Well, God, I don't . . ."

"Do this," Bolan urged, still trying to talk him clear. "First, cool your head. You can't work the problem if you don't have a head. Then keep the date with Eritrea. Make a play, and take no decisions whatever until you can evaluate the results of that play. At that moment, Leo, you'll do what you have to do. But give it that much. Give it that much, guy!"

Those tortured eyes were beginning to settle down. It had been a long, hard "life" for this little guy. Bolan's heart was squeezed for him.

"Thanks," Leo said a moment later. He got up

and started off but then turned back with an empty, cockeyed smile. "Just so you'll know, Sarge. I have a hollow tooth. And I have a pill that fits that tooth. I just want you to know. I'll never be a turkey."

Bolan groaned, "*God*, Leo."

The best friend he'd ever had walked up the aisle and out of view.

Bolan had not felt such emotion for a long time. It was threatening, now, to burst out all over him.

That's the way, he knew, when a guy lived forever at tight rein. He could imagine, then, the inner forces now tearing at Leo Turrin.

The worst of it, from Bolan's inner view, was that he felt chiefly responsible for this sorry development. He'd talked the guy into stonewalling the Pittsfield purge. *This*—this right now—was the "boilover" which Bolan himself had so diligently sought. And so it had come to this. Full capitulation for Leo, with no alternative remotely in sight.

Probably as bad as any other feature was the unhappy fact that a *mafioso's* wife had been snatched out of a government safe house. Her presence therein, in the mob view, could mean but one thing. Well—one of two things. Leo Turrin had made a deal with the feds—or he was a fed himself. Either way, there would be no comfort for Leo or his wife.

Bolan felt absolutely wretched.

Once again, also, the "iron man" was reminded of why he himself had opted for the solitary life. He'd turned away from his only blood, his kid brother, and he'd turned away also from the first woman he had ever truly loved—simply to avoid this sort of situation. The Bolan name was lost forever. Young Johnny had been the last of the line—

124

and now he was living the secret life in a western state under an assumed name.

Yeah. He felt wretched. It was a sorry goddamned excuse for living, this solitary adventure into damnation.

But, looking at Leo Turrin's disappearing back, Mack Bolan was glad that he was alone.

One day—perhaps this very day—he would die alone.

But a lot of others were going to get there ahead of him. Mack Bolan himself had reached the flashpoint. The Executioner was in "boilover" mode. He got up and took his leave—with a final, almost yearning look toward the ladies. And, yeah—he decided—the basic difference there lay in an orientation to the life process.

Most *men*, it seemed, were oriented toward death.

# CHAPTER FIFTEEN

## Alignments

"This is Striker. Leo is too numb to lay it out. What happened?"

The headfed was obviously in about the same mood as Bolan. That voice was strained almost to its limits as it came back along the clean line. "We found our leak, the hard way. That's what happened. I'm going to crucify a certain Senate aide with this one, bet on that. And if I can't crucify him then I'll get satisfaction with my own penknife at his balls!"

"That won't save the situation, Hal. Stop beating yourself. The only thing you're guilty of is moral optimism in a world gone crazy. What are you doing to save it?"

"I have fifty federal marshals sifting through everything from cobwebs in the attic to the sand on the beach. And I am very seriously contemplating an FBI raid on the New York headshed. I'm going in within minutes for authorization for a complete sweep of the entire eastern seaboard. I'll make it so goddamned hot for these cocky bastards they won't *dare* rearrange a hair of that lady's head! I'll—"

"You won't get it, you know. The authorization. All you'll get is a waltz around the White House ballroom. So forget it."

"Forget it, *hell*! They can have my resignation if—"

"Hal! You're not thinking! Stop beating yourself, dammit, and start thinking! Who got snatched? The president's wife? Hell no! A little Italian housewife who's married to an undercover operative whose very existence is already an embarrassment to the federal executive—that's who got snatched! Now forget that!"

It was pretty strong talk for a man of Brognola's high office but it seemed to have an immediate shock value, if nothing else. The line was silent for perhaps ten seconds. When the headfed got himself back together, the mood was stiff and cool, but decidedly more thoughtful.

"I wish you had to sit in this chair for just twenty-four hours, Striker. Would you like to trade? I'll make the switch tonight—right now."

Bolan replied, "No way. You've got your cross and I've got mine. Let's hook them together for awhile and see if we can't lighten the load on both."

The guy heaved an overlong sigh, then told the most wanted man in America: "You're right. Okay. You're also entirely right about the little Italian housewife. So I guess I'm open to suggestions. Do you have one—from your cross to mine?"

"Leo is trying to work something cool from this end," Bolan reported. "Let's give it a couple of hours and see what he can flush through. Meanwhile there is something you should be working. The other problem, Hal."

"Which other problem?"

"The cover problem. They snatched the lady out of a government house. I don't have to spell that out, do I."

"There's no way to save it. Short of mass assas-

128

sinations, I guess—and I don't even know the candidates. They found the lady through our Senate leak. Now they could not have known *who* they had found, not by name, not until after the actual snatch. All they learned from here was that we were safing the family of a very important government operative who is getting ready to break cover and enter the courts. But they know, now, Striker. They have to know now."

"What happened to the men you had with her?"

Brognola sighed. "They'll be buried the day after tomorrow."

Bolan said, "I believe your first idea was the best. Do you know for sure who the guy is?"

"Not in any sense of hard legal evidence, no. My gut knows for sure, though."

"Okay, grab the guy. To hell with due process. Grab the guy and take him to a sweat room. Beat hell out of him, scare him out of his skull—do whatever it takes—but find out what his alignment is. Don't tell me you can't do that."

"With all my strong talk," Brognola admitted, "the very soul cringes at the thought."

"You're dealing with savages, Hal. You can't civilize them overnight. Take the guy to the fire. We've got a matter of hours and we need to make the most of every minute there is. You let your conscience be your guide and if it leads you into the right corners of your cringing soul then you hit my floater as soon as you get a name and you leave the goddamn message—and leave the burden on *my* smarting soul! Tell me no!"

Brognola sighed the sigh of the damned. "You know I can't. Okay. Soon as I know something, you'll get the flash."

"Now you're thinking," Bolan growled, and hung it up, and went on to the next alignment.

Bolan's new face had never been inside this place; still, the high-risk factor was very real any time Mack Bolan walked into a police station. Artist's sketches of the "new look" had been circulated worldwide. Right here in the home town, the "penetration" was doubly daring. The man he sought was a man who had come to know the young Sergeant Bolan quite well—and any man was more than a mere face.

But this one was for the marbles.

He left the car at the curb in a ten-minute zone, donned smoked glasses, and went inside. He showed federal credentials at the desk and told the pretty lady there, "I was asked to check in with Captain Weatherbee."

She gave him a pretty smile and an invitation to rest in a soft chair while he waited—and she kept throwing him quick smiles until that final one which sent him up the stairs to "the second door on the right."

The big cop had put on a few more big pounds; otherwise he looked about the same as a captain as he'd looked as a lieutenant—that same solemn expression which could vary in a twink from sour to sweet, those same piercing eyes that saw everything and revealed nothing—a one-hundred-percent cop, who would not know how to live any other life.

Bolan shook hands and flashed the Washington ID as both men murmured say-nothing greetings, then he went to the window to stand with the light behind him as he looked onto the street. "Nice town," he said, as though speaking to himself.

"First visit to our town, uh, Pulaski is it?"

"Not exactly," Bolan muttered. He turned back to the cop but kept the window behind him, framing himself in the bright sunlight so that the contrast would be all in his favor. "You handled the thing at the airport very nicely. We appreciate it."

The captain was giving him that reveal-nothing police appraisal. "Haven't we met before?"

"Possibly. This is my first time through here in quite awhile, though. People change, you know."

"They do at that, don't they." The big cop seemed to be losing interest in the small talk. He lit a cigar and spoke around it as he inquired, "What can I do for the federal government this afternoon?"

"This is straight down the pike, Captain. A lot of hell is headed this way."

"It got here already," Weatherbee sniffed. His hand gesture took in a confusion of glossy photos which littered his desk. "We're still trying to put it together."

"By nightfall, you'll have forgotten that even happened," Bolan said coldly. "The New York bunch is fielding a battalion force. It's on the way here right now."

The captain did not bat an eye. "So why aren't you heading them off at the pass?"

"Too little and too late, that's why. I wanted to alert you to the fact that—"

"Okay, I'm alerted. The City of Pittsfield thanks you. Now why don't you get the hell out of our town, hotrocks, and take all the hell with you."

Bolan removed his glasses, dropped into a chair, and sent the guy a very solemn smile. "You had me going in, didn't you," he said quietly.

131

The cop did not return the smile. The expression in those eyes were—if anything at all was readable—pained. "New face and all, you've got a hell of a nerve—I'll say that. What makes you think you'll be allowed to walk out of here?"

"I had to take the chance, Al. Too much is going down."

Weatherbee harrumped and said, "Should've thought of that before you came. I warned you before and I'm warning you again. You're into something you can't possibly handle to a conclusion. There's only one possible end to it. New face and all, mister, you are just so much dead meat awaiting burial." The harsh gaze relented somewhat as the stern old cop added, "Still, I guess you're about the most man I've ever run into. I'll give you five minutes, soldier boy—then I'm suddenly going to place that altered face."

Bolan told him, "I'll take four of them right here."

The guy actually smiled. He said, "Always pushing, aren't you. Is that badge you showed me for real?"

Bolan shook his head and formed a "no" with his lips. "Comes in kind of handy from time to time, though."

"Not here, buddy-o. So they're sending you a battalion force. Just what is a battalion force?"

"Several hundred guns. Helicopters. ATV's. Probably some exotic weaponry. Maybe even some dogs."

Weatherbee grunted and swiped at his nose with a finger. "Sounds like a paramilitary force."

"It is."

"Then you'd better be getting along, hadn't you."

132

"I was hoping you would get with the county and state, talk them into putting up some roadblocks. Maybe close off a few area airfields. That sort of thing."

"Why would I do that? I don't even know they're coming."

"You know I'm leaving."

Those police eyes lay all over Bolan for about thirty seconds before the old cop replied, "That's what you really want?"

Bolan shrugged. "It's one problem at a time with me, Captain. Right now my problem is a battalion force. I doubt that anything will stop them completely. But I'll need all the time you can buy me."

Weatherbee slowly shook his head. "You really want them bad, don't you, soldier boy. How much is it going to take to sate you, youngster? Haven't you drunk enough blood to wipe out all the sins of the world?"

"You make it sound like some sort of feast."

"Vengeance always is, isn't it?"

It was Bolan's turn to lay eyes all over. Finally he said, "Think what you like." He stood up. "Guess my four minutes are gone."

"I had to ask it," Weatherbee said amiably. "I've been having this debate with Alice. Alice is my wife. I guess she sees something in you that reminds her of Jack Armstrong, the all-American boy. I've been telling her it doesn't usually work that way in real life. So if it's not vengeance, what is it? What is it about you that gets a tough goat like Hal Brognola all lathered up every time you stub a toe? What is it that causes good honest cops all over this country to turn their backs and look the other way when they see you walking by?"

Bolan paused at the door and sort of half-looked at the guy. "About those roadblocks . . ."

"I'll try."

"What is it?" Bolan asked quietly, "about a tough old cop who never took a pad in his life that makes him enter a conspiracy with the most wanted criminal in the country?"

He stepped into the hall and collided with another cop—a youngish guy with a burly body and baby face.

"Hi, Pappas," Bolan said easily and went on out of there.

"Who was that?" Sergeant Pappas asked the captain as he stepped into the office.

Weatherbee sighed and clasped his hands behind his back. "That," he said solemnly, "was Jack Armstrong."

"I thought he looked—who the hell is Jack Armstrong?"

"I guess you're too young to know, Johnny boy. It's a flaming anachronism, a vanishing species of American life."

"I don't know what you're talking about, Cap. The guy called me by name. How'd he know my name?"

"That guy," Weatherbee said, eyes twinkling, "sees all, knows all, and, I guess, does all."

"I don't get you."

"You just bumped into Mack Bolan, Johnny. Better sound the alarm. He's probably already gotten away clean."

Long before the flustered Sergeant Pappas could "sound the alarm," the flaming anachronism was indeed "away clean."

But he had another stop to make, on the way

134

out of town. He needed to see a man about a man. He had to insure Leo Turrin's realignment. He wanted to have a quiet little talk with David Eritrea.

# CHAPTER SIXTEEN

## Macho Machismo

David and Leo were behind closed doors in a super-private conference. Angelo Flavia sat by the window with a newspaper, Tamiano and another boy were watching an old movie on TV, turned way down low—and the punchy little tagman, Fresni, was boring holes in Billy Gino with his eyes.

Billy shifted uncomfortably in his chair at the door, wishing Fresni would look at something else for awhile. What the hell did the guy think Billy was going to do—crash in there and start blasting away at his boss?

He was almost happy to get the beep on his radio. He yanked the antenna up and growled, "Yeah, what is it?"

"We got a visitor, Billy," came a report from the hallway station. "You better come."

He called Tamiano away from his movie to relieve him at the door, gave a sympathetic smile to Fresni, and went out to see who was calling.

A tall guy wearing dark eyeshades and a five-hundred-dollar suit was standing with three boys in the elevator, casually talking about something that was just delighting the hell out of his listeners. It was a hell of a way to conduct a security watch and Billy Gino was very unhappy with his people until one of them jogged up the hall to meet him with the excited whisper, "It's a Black Ace, Billy. He came to find Leo Turrin."

So that explained it.

Billy Gino felt his hackles rising as he ambled on toward the clutch at the elevator. An Ace of Spades, also called Black Ace, was something very special in the organization. Those guys were the elite of the elite. You did not see them on every street corner—hell, not on *any* street corner. You rarely saw them, even, in that fancy highrise in midtown Manhattan. Billy Gino could not include the Black Aces in the contempt he held for the usual cadre of *Commissione* hotshots. There were Aces and then there were Black Aces. The Blacks were the top of the cut, man. You just naturally had to respect those guys. There was no other way to take them.

His own boys on the elevator detail looked as though they would be willing to strew rose petals or something in the guy's path. He had them thoroughly charmed. No frozen-faced robots, these guys. These guys were solid *class*, all the way through, and they knew how to come on properly to the working stiffs.

As Billy Gino approached within earshot, the guy was just finishing some funny story. "... jumped out of that third story window with his clothes wrapped around his neck. That's the last I saw of Tommy Domencio—and that's the last the lady saw of him, too."

The boys were guffawing it up and didn't even know their boss was there. The Black Ace knew it, though. He flicked a sidewise glance Billy's way and stuck out a hand. "Hi, Billy. What are you doing so far from home?"

138

Billy Gino shook the Ace's hand and tried not to look too interested. "We uh—when did we meet?"

The guy grinned at him as he replied, "Oh, now and then, Billy. You don't always know it, but I do."

Billy Gino could believe that. These guys were like ghosts, always around but hardly ever visible. It was really a rare event to actually be standing here and jawing with one. It was whispered on the streets that the Black Aces had committed to memory the entire life history and present circumstances of every made man in the organization, and knew them intimately—even to the type of women they preferred and their favorite positions in bed. That was an exaggeration of course, but it did reflect rather accurately the awe in which these guys were held by the street soldiers.

And why not? They were every soldier's dream of perfection—the ultimate man, Mr. Macho, who could mingle with any and be at complete ease with all. These guys were the powers behind the throne—and all knew it.

Billy Gino did not buy it all that strongly—but he had to admit that he was affected by the *machismo* of these guys. This one was no exception. Those eyes were hardly visible behind the smoked glass, but Billy Gino knew that they were there and dissecting him thoroughly, sizing and measuring him even as the guy handed over the little ID folder and said, "Call me Omega. I need to see Leo Turrin. It's very urgent. Give my respects to David, but send Leo out."

Billy barely looked at the shiny, specially embossed plastic playing card in the wallet. It was an Ace of Spades, all right—and it was the only ID the guys carried. It was enough.

Billy said, "Won't you step inside, sir? I'm sure Mr. Eritrea would want to say hello. He's in a, uh, very urgent conference with Mr. Turrin right now. But I'm sure—"

The guy had a hand on Billy's shoulder and they were already strolling up the hall toward the suite. Billy could not decide which of them had started first, it was that smooth. The Ace of Spades was telling him, "It's a tense time, Billy, and I don't want to spend any unnecessarily. I do have some unhappy news for Leo, though, so I'm afraid I'm going to have to bust in on them."

"Oh, say, I'm sure they wouldn't mind a bit."

Billy was falling under the guy's spell—and he knew it and hated himself for it—but, dammit, there it was. The word had already spread, too. Some of the boys were standing in their open doorways, some with nothing but a towel cinched about the waist, just to get a look at the guy. That embarrassed Billy Gino. He felt the need to apologize for the behavior of his boys, but he didn't quite know how to put it without making things worse.

He lamely explained, "We have the whole floor, you know. So we can leave the doors open and just let the boys wander around some. Kind of takes away the four walls feeling. You know what I mean. A guy can go stir crazy in a hotel room."

The guy chuckled and assured Billy that he knew what Billy meant. And he was calling out names as he passed the doorways, saying things like "Watch those Swedish women, Jerry," and "How's the action on Lexington Avenue, Eddie?"

It went over real big, and Billy Gino was getting a real demonstration of how legends were born. Nothing, it seemed, more impressed a soldier of the streets than having a bigshot recognize him on sight and say something intimately personal to him.

One of the greatest things—Billy knew it so well—was to have cadre loyalty so fierce that a boy would gladly die for his boss, without even questioning why. Billy had been able to feel that in only three or four boys during all his years as bodycock. This guy had it already, with one pass along the hall. Those goddamn dumb boys would die for the guy who called them by name and mentioned something personal in their lives, however vague it might be.

Billy recognized this curious street psychology even while acknowledging that he himself was susceptible to it. He had swelled with strange emotion when the guy stuck out that paw and said, "Hi, Billy—what're you doing so far from home?"

The guy knew his name and where he came from—and Billy Gino had swelled up immediately.

The knowledge irritated him just a bit, but he still ushered the guy into the suite with a restrained flourish and went very quickly to that closed door at the far end of the room. He was a bit flustered, though, to find the guy right beside him when he reached that door; he thought he'd left the guy up front, and he became aware of the presence alongside only when Jocko Fresni leapt to attention and the guy called over to him, "Hey, Jocko, what was your score?"

The little dumbo glowed as he replied, "I won two games and had to walk off and leave 'em." And he did not even make a fuss when Billy rapped on the door and went in alone.

David growled, "What's all the fuss, Billy?"

Billy handed over the ID wallet and said, "He's

called Omega. He came to see Mr. Turrin. Says it's urgent."

David tossed a surprised look at Turrin and asked him, "Do you know this Omega?"

The Pittsfield boss replied, "Yeah, sort of, I think." His glance swept to Billy Gino. "Tall guy, very smooth and *macho*?"

Billy nodded dumbly to that. Hell, they all looked that way. "He says he has some unhappy news for you, Mr. Turrin."

Turrin took the wallet from David and went quickly to the door. David got up and slowly followed, glancing at himself in a wall mirror as he passed it. That embarrassed Billy. David shouldn't give a damn about—well, maybe he should. Even full bosses behaved differently, it was said, with an Ace of Spades on the premises.

David sort of hung there just inside the door, as though he could not decide whether he should just go on out or wait for the guy to come in.

Obviously, though, the guy was not coming in. Billy moved into the open doorway and announced, a bit too loudly, "Mr. Eritrea, this is Mr. Omega."

David took the cue and came out with his hand ready—but Omega was busy with something else. He was busy taking over. He jabbed a stiff finger toward Billy Gino and Jocko Fresni, saying, "You boys stay. You other boys catch some air. Not you, Angelo—you stay, too." Then, without even taking a breath, he reached over to grab David's dangling hand and said, "Sorry to butt in this way, David. Pardon me just a minute." Then he left David standing there with a dumb look on his face and pulled the little Pittsfield boss into a tight conference in a far corner of the room.

The "other boys" hurried out of the room.

"What the hell is this?" David said furiously, but not very loudly.

"I'm sure it's nothing personal, Mr. Eritrea," Billy said quickly, leaping into the breach even while wondering why he was apologizing for the guy.

What the hell *was* going on here?

# CHAPTER SEVENTEEN

## Brokering

"You're crazy!" Leo whispered furiously. "What the hell are you—?"

"Shut up and listen," Bolan said calmly. "I talked to Hal. We have a play onstage and things are looking much brighter than they may appear. I'm going to put an arm on Eritrea, here and now. But I need to know how far you've gone with him."

"Pretty far," Leo replied uneasily. "The guy is trying to bind me to him. Just about like you said."

"What's his offer?"

"Domain. Claims he has DiAnglia and the other New York bosses behind him. Says they're getting ready for a showdown and they're making the cut very soon. Says they like my style and hope they can count on me for some quick support. What do you think?"

"Did he mention Augie?"

"Not hardly, no."

"Did you ask?"

"Not directly. I asked how Augie was doing. He said Augie is doing fine, but planning for the future. I think that was meant as a hint that Augie is naming David as heir apparent and wants to insure support for him, from beyond the grave."

"Uh huh. Okay. Let's play that."

"I'm game."

"Let your true feeling hang out, Leo. Right now. I've just notified you that Angelina was snatched."

The little guy took a quick step backwards and raised his voice to cry out, "*What?*"

Fresni had been skulking about in the distant background. He scrambled to a stiff, toe-stretching stance and yelled up, "Leo? You okay?"

"I'm okay!" Turrin snarled. "Just relax!" He punched the wall and kicked a pillow off the sofa.

"Save it!" Bolan said loudly. "We'll put it to work where it will do some good!"

Eritrea and Gino cautiously drifted over. Leo turned his back to them and walked stiffly to the window to stare down onto the street.

"What the hell is it?" Eritrea asked softly.

"We need to talk, David," Bolan told him.

The guy took his arm and gently pulled him along. "Sure. Back here. Come on. Billy—get some refreshments."

"Coffee's fine," Bolan said sourly.

"Me too, Billy. Get some fresh stuff up from the kitchen."

Bolan allowed himself to be piloted to the back room. He kicked the door shut as he passed through and turned immediately to his host. "This is entirely confidential, David."

"Oh, sure."

The guy was trying to get Bolan into a chair. Instead, he went to the window and struck a pose there, looking back at the guy with a sober smile. "I really came to see you."

"Sure. I understand."

"I came as soon as I could. How bad were you hurt?"

"Bad enough. We lost half the force. Leo says Bolan is in town—and the cops are saying the

146

same thing. I figured it was Leo who sprang us at the airport. Leo says uh-uh, it wasn't him. Says he smells Bolan all over that hit."

"Leo should know. The guy has been through the fire."

"Right. He should know."

"It wasn't all Bolan, David."

"Yes, I, uh—why the hell did the guy mix in that way? He saved my ass, you know. I can't figure why."

The "Black Ace" shrugged his shoulders as he replied, "Don't try to figure that guy. He gets pretty cutesy, sometimes. I think you've seen the last of him for awhile. I stopped off to see Weatherbee on the way over here."

"Who?—oh! You, uh, have a thing with the guy?"

Bolan wagged his hand. "Off and on. The cops figure the town suddenly got too hot for Bolan. I agree with that. Anyway, Bolan isn't your problem right now."

"Who is? Do you know?"

Bolan jerked his head at the door. "One of them is right out there. Work it right and you'll have a loyal compadre for life. I say that with full knowledge of the guy."

"You said a problem. Work what right?"

"I just brought the guy some rotten news. Did he tell you what's been going on down here?"

Eritrea jerked his head in a quick nod. "Someone contracted him. I think I can work—"

"That's only part of the problem. I just brought him the other part. They snatched his wife."

Eritrea's eyes jerked. "That's a lousy . . ."

"Lousier than you know. They tried to dirty the guy, in the bargain. They worked a con through a dirt merchant in Washington. Dummied up a gov-

147

ernment safe house and knocked off a couple of feds. The news will break later tonight that Leo's woman was in that safe house."

Eritrea's eyes were working the problem. He said, "Slick, mighty slick. They've got the poor guy coming and going, haven't they."

Bolan sighed. He stared through the window for a moment, then turned back to his patsy. "Maybe and maybe not. They're trying to get a tab on the guy, that's all. It doesn't have to work, David."

"I see what you mean."

"Here's what you're to do."

"Okay."

"Get it back down to the Big Apple. Take Leo with you. Get your council together and make the cut. Lay it out flat. They come in on the top of the cut or they get the hell out. You'll have my full support, and I speak for several others. You know what I mean."

The guy could not suppress the smile. He said, "That's very warming. I can't tell you how much I—"

"Forget it. I'm just doing my job. I don't like what I've been seeing lately—and I'm not the only one. So we put it together. And we came down on your side of the cut. We want you to know that—and to act accordingly. It's mainly why I'm here right now."

"Yes, that's very warming. I would need to be able to count on that support, you know. There is a very powerful opposition, as you must know."

"Don't worry about that opposition. It's another reason I'm here. Your opposition won't have any teeth by the time you get back home."

"Hey, Omega, I can't tell you—I just can't express . . ."

The guy was too overwhelmed to express his gratitude.

Bolan was giving him a smug smile. "All you have to do now, David, is make your move."

"Okay. That's great. What about Augie?"

Bolan was still showing the smug smile. "Yeah. What about him?"

Eritrea fairly beamed. "Fine. Just so we understand."

Boland did not, but he did not let it show. "You'll have to see to Leo's problems. Don't let it undo you. If they get away with that stuff—well, it could hurt you."

"Maybe I should just cut the guy away right now."

Bolan shook his head, displeasure showing plainly. "I wouldn't advise that. You know how word gets out. It would make you look weak. Shove it back down their dirty throats, David."

The guy was beaming again. "I will. Count on it. I will. I know how to do it."

Bolan was sure he did.

He said, "Okay. Do what you can to get his woman back and shove the dirt back down their lousy throats in the bargain. It's important, in more ways than one. Leo is a popular guy with some of us. We don't like what they're doing to him. I guess maybe that's what finally tipped it. So that benefit goes to you, as well. Don't mess it up, David."

"Don't worry about it. I feel the same way about Leo. He's a valuable man. We can't afford that kind of loss."

"Right. We feel the same about you, David."

"Well—I appreciate that. We're going to have a

149

much stronger organization, after this. I'll want to get very close with your people."

"That goes with the cut. Right? How soon can you get moving?"

Eritrea glanced at his watch. "Well, hell, what's to—I'll have to square it with Weatherbee."

"Leave that to me."

"Fine. I guess I can line up a charter. I really hadn't thought yet about—"

"Why don't you let Leo get you some cars? You can be there in a couple of hours."

"Right. We'll do it that way."

"We're depending on you, David."

Bolan was walking toward the door. He took the guy by the arm and steered him along.

"When you get back, get with DiAnglia right away and clue him in. Tell him what we're doing. He should load the streets and make some noise so there's no misreading of the signals."

"Right. I'll do that."

They stepped through the doorway and into the sitting room. Billy Gino was just then wheeling in a room service table loaded with coffee and pastries.

"Tell Billy," Bolan suggested. "Tell him, also, I've had an eye on him. Tell him there are good things ahead for him."

Eritrea beamed and said, "He's a hell of a good man."

"He's *Commissione* material," Bolan suggested.

"So is Leo, come to think of it," Eritrea said proudly.

"That's an idea," Bolan said. "Why don't you try it on him? On your way down, maybe. Feel him out."

"Right, I'll do that."

"I'll just want to give the poor guy an encouraging word before I go."

"Good idea," Eritrea said.

Bolan strolled across the room toward Leo Turrin. Eritrea crossed immediately to Billy Gino.

"What are you doing?" Leo hissed.

"Playing the game," Bolan said quietly.

"Yeah, but what game?"

"Brokering. I believe the alignment is secure, Leo. Don't worry about Angelina. She's going to be okay. So are you. You're going to the city with Eritrea and company. Play it for all it's worth."

"Wait a minute! What are you—?"

"I'll clean it up here and quietly fade over the horizon. Omega will take a new face and a new name—and nobody will ever be the wiser. Smile, buddy. You're about to become a commissioner."

"You're crazy!"

"Sure I am. So are you. But so are all of *them*. So what's the difference? Play the game, Leo. And keep it tucked tight."

He spun on his toe and walked away from the double-lifer with the hollow tooth and the death pill to fit.

Sure. They were all crazy as loons.

# CHAPTER EIGHTEEN

## Romancing

The thing was moving entirely to Bolan's liking, now. He could feel the pace flowing past the quivering war tendrils of his soldier's mind and he knew—the same as every soldier always knows, when that moment arrives—that the balance between life and death was weighting his every move.

He put in a quick call to Al Weatherbee to ask the cop: "How's your conscience?"

"Never felt better. The chief has set an emergency meeting to discuss the unsettled conditions here. State will be there and so will county—even a few FBI people, I'm told. He's going to push for an immediate clampdown to seal this town off tight. But it works both ways, buddy-o."

"It's still good news, Al. Thanks."

The guy sighed as he said, "Play your cards right, maybe it will buy you one more ride around the gravesite. But you still know where you're headed, don't you."

Bolan told him, "We're all headed there, aren't we. I just elected to pick my own route. By the way, I have some good news for you, too. The hard luck kids are breaking camp at this moment and calling it quits. I think you should let them pass unchallenged, and good riddance."

"How do you know they're leaving?"

153

"Because someone told Eritrea that's what he should do and he agreed with the logic. I also told him I'd let you know."

"I don't believe it," Weatherbee sniffed.

"Don't believe it, then. But Al—let them go."

"That isn't what I didn't believe. I was being cute. Guess I'm too old for cute."

"You?" Bolan said, chuckling. "Never. Bet you'd never sell that idea to Alice."

"Oh, she thinks I'm pretty cute. Sometimes. Tonight she's going to think I'm Rudolf Valentino. Or, better yet, what's that guy with the round table and the shining armor?"

Bolan hung up chuckling and immediately placed another call. Billy Gino took it. Bolan told him, "It's me, Billy. Tell David I squared it with Weatherbee. You should be on your way within thirty minutes, though. They're sealing the town. That's all the time you're going to have."

"Yes sir, okay. Thanks, mister—"

"You call me Omega, Billy."

"Say, listen, David told me what you said. You're an okay guy, Omega. From now on, you just tell Billy Gino where and what and when. You know what I mean."

"I appreciate that, Billy," the "Ace" replied solemnly and hung up.

Sure, he knew what Billy Gino meant. It was a pledge of fealty to the grave. Bolan shook his head and went to his vehicle, thinking about all the Billy Ginos everywhere. Such a lot of waste for so little a cause. Where would the world be, he wondered, if all that fierce loyalty could be properly harnessed by the right leaders and put to work for something positive in the world?

He set off for the north hills knowing that such

an occurrence was not likely in any forseeable future. There were just not those kinds of leaders around. As for the Billy Ginos of the world . . . Bolan had forever marveled at the curious fact that these guys were really hard core romanticists. They gave devotion and commitment to the grave because the idea fit some deep sense of rightness in their romantic souls. For a similar reason, other men sometimes robbed and killed or committed heinous crimes—romantic souls in rebellion against the humdrum life. The nation's prisons were full of such men.

All were not savages, Bolan decided then and there. Some had simply seen the fire—and paused there to wonder what it meant, how it worked, and whether they could snatch up a small firebrand and carry it along with them through the darkness.

Yeah, Bolan understood such men. Not that he agreed with them—but he understood.

The ones he would never understand were the David Eritrea types. Their problem was precisely the opposite. They had no romance, no soul—and they had never seen the fire. Savages, yes, in the classic sense. All savages were not criminals, either. They could be found in the shops and mills and corporate offices and police stations and legislatures, as well. Yet they were as savage in their effect upon the world as any gun-crazy hood on any street in the land. The corrupt politicos and bureaucrats, the power-crazy corporate executives and ambitious young climbers of every ilk who felt through dead souls for some symbol of manhood and crushed everything noble before them in their sterile reach for potency without romance, domain without humility, wealth without compassion—there was savagery run rampant, right there.

155

Yeah. And it made Bolan sick to think about it. Those savages were as clear and present an enemy—however invisible and "legal"—as any Mack Bolan had gone against.

But, hell, Bolan did not fancy himself wearing a cross for the world—the remark to Brognola notwithstanding—and certainly he did not seek to atone for the sins of all through the blood of a few, whatever Weatherbee may have chosen to believe. Too many "saviours" had died for this tired world already. Bolan did not *die* for the gentle world, dammit. The same as he desired for Leo Turrin he desired for himself. He wanted to *live* for the world—but to make that life count for something noble and good and—yes, dammit—and *romantic*.

It was the romantic male, with his basic orientation toward the process called *death*, who provided *joy* for the ladies' bowling league. That was Bolan's illumination—female lib to hell and back. A man was a man and a woman was something else—yet the one was not a damn thing without the other. And the male with no romance in his soul was not a damn thing to begin with.

The war drums were in Bolan's pulse, now. The hardsite was just around the next curve. He pushed all else from his mind, tensed into the combat ready, and sallied forth into the fire.

With, yeah, romance in his soul.

# CHAPTER NINETEEN

## The Probe

He moved the vehicle smoothly along the gently ascending drive at a steady pace, then picked up speed in the straightaway as he crossed the periphery of the auto-fire zone.

It was going to be very tricky, sure.

One hand was at the door as he maneuvered past the shattered area which had once marked the gateway to new empire in America.

And then his corner vision caught the motion as, high above and far away, a tiny flash of light leapt from the background of trees and lifted in brilliance as a long tail of flame and smoke began marking the fiery path of the target track.

Bolan flung himself from the vehicle and sent it careening along without a pilot as he took cover in the earlier wreckage. Four numbers later the paths of rocket and automobile converged at the doomsday point, the rocket screaming overhead and finding its mark with a flash and a roar that sucked at Bolan's flesh and pummeled the bones inside.

He was up and running for the house even as the fireball continued to expand.

"Hold your fire!" he yelled at the top of his lungs as he reached the front lawn and sprinted for the porch.

A door flew open and Bolan dived through the opening, then lay there panting as energetic others grabbed at him and rolled him over. A foot landed harshly atop his belly, another on his throat, and the twin barrels of a sawed-off shotgun yawned in his face.

"Breast pocket!" he grunted.

A hand flipped the coat back and hauled out the wallet, another took the Beretta Belle out of the shoulder harness.

Instantly, then, the feet were removed from his body and a concerned voice chuckled, "Hey, that was great, what a hell of a great run that was!"

Helpful hands pulled him to his feet and dusted his five-hundred-dollar threads, then fell respectfully back at a distance.

The one with the chuckly voice returned the Beretta but retained the ID wallet. "No disrespect, sir. That was really great. How the *hell* did you get out of that?"

The demolished car was no more than a hundred feet downrange. The red glow from the flames that consumed it danced at the windows and sent wild shadows playing on the walls of the great room. Hushed men stood at those windows and marveled at the destructive power unleashed in their presence.

Another guy appeared. A bit shorter than Bolan, a bit heavier, a bit younger—if there was any way to really figure age from one of those frozen faces. "Yes, just how *did* you get out of that?" Simon inquired in that curiously stilted speech.

"Saw the damn thing coming," Bolan grunted. "That is one hell of a shocking sight, Simon."

The guy may have grinned; Bolan could not be sure. "Your eyes are as good as your legs," he said.

"Pure luck," Bolan said modestly. "I saw the wreckage at the gate. I was looking around to see why. I saw why."

"Did you see where it came from?"

"Up in the hills, there, to the west."

The guy nodded his head and reached for the ID wallet. He glanced at it and turned it back to Bolan. He was outranked. This showed immediately in the new formality. He said, "You have me at a disadvantage."

Bolan glanced at the fire and grinned. "Call me Lucky," he said.

The guy grinned back—a real grin, this time. "I'm glad you're here, but I'm sorry you had so much trouble getting in. We have this little problem, you know." He turned to Chuckles with a harsh look. "There was no need to rough him up that way. You should have seen the man was running for his life."

The chuckler apologized.

Bolan said, "It's okay. I should have called ahead."

Simon was seething with questions, but the respect for protocol kept them all inside. Instead, he offered refreshments.

Bolan declined, and told him, "Battalion will be a bit delayed."

The guy's eyes twitched, but no emotion moved that frozen face. "I hope not for long."

"Just a bit of rerouting. This territory is suddenly very hot. I'll need to tell the man."

The guy gestured toward the stairway. They walked shoulder to shoulder through the big room. Bolan quick-counted about thirty heads in there. The place was pretty much as Leo had described it, though not so "plush" in its revival. Very plain

159

and obviously new furniture was scattered about. The men here wore the grim look of "siege," and the morale was obviously not high. The chuckler was apparently a crew boss. He was pushing the guys away from the windows and trying to settle them down.

All the doors upstairs stood open, but one. Leo had said "a large suite," and this had to be it.

Bolan was hoping to find more than "the man" behind that closed door. A wild hunch had prompted this very risky penetration of the new empire; a gut-shaking hunch, however, and there was no alternative but to check it out.

He hoped to find Angelina Turrin behind that door.

Simon requested, "Wait here, please." He brushed his knuckles against the wood and pushed inside.

Bolan stood casually in the hall, playing it cool, framed in the open doorway and displaying little interest in what lay beyond that doorway until he would be bidden to enter.

But the bid did not come.

Instead, a heavy voice from the interior rumbled, "That's Mack Bolan! Take him!"

The following few seconds were a dizzying procession of oddly disoriented events, as survival instincts flared with combat-consciousness of instant crisis.

This was where conditioning always met the test.

The Beretta was in Bolan's hand chugging penciled flame through that doorway, even as his thinking mind clutched at the edges of reality and sent him spinning along that hall and into the only possible route of flight. He hit the window at the end of the hall at full gallop and crashed on through with only the vaguest perception of what lay below.

It was highly fortunate that what lay below was the low sloping roof above the kitchen entrance. Bolan landed there in an instinctive crouch, legs doubled beneath him and flexing into the push-off for the next level below.

He hit the ground in a rolling drop and found his feet without loss of forward motion. A chopper cut loose on him from an upstairs window just as he rounded the corner to temporary safety and opened the stride toward happier turf.

But then from nowhere a shotgun ba-loomed and sent him spinning to the grass on both knees as the charge caught his flapping coat and tore it away from him. He experienced sudden pain but no disability as he twisted on and sent a Parabellum sizzler along the backtrack, targeting purely by instinct. He heard an immediate telltale grunt and saw the shotgun tumbling to earth—and again, somehow, he was on his feet and sprinting past the bungalows, while frenzied gunshots erupted along various quarters of the backtrack.

A vision only half glimpsed and foggily perceived tugged at a corner of his mind as he put the bungalows behind him and hurdled the fence. He was in cover, now, trees and shrubbery, and he knew that it was half made.

Better than that, even.

A voice from the house screamed, "It's enough! Let 'im go! Nobody crosses the fence!"

A super-cautious force, sure.

Which suited an ex-Black Ace just fine.

He'd tried the cute routine once too often and found a place where it would not take. Why not? Whose voice? Was there something familiar?—

161

something recognizable in that coarse bellow? No. Nothing to bet a life on.

He moved on, slowly now, stuffing breath back in and exploring hurts. A leg was a bit trembly and there was some raw flesh across the back where the coat had been, but he was not bleeding appreciably and he was not dead.

It had been a "great run" at both ends of that trip.

And it was good enough. The probe had paid for itself. He had not seen into that darkened room, and he had not recognized that voice of crisis.

He had, however, come away with what he'd gone in there to get. He'd come away with a vision half glimpsed and foggily perceived—but now, with the crisis ended, suddenly jarringly in focus—a vision of a naked lady huddled miserably against the wall of a bare room in that end bungalow.

Uh huh. He'd found Angelina.

# CHAPTER TWENTY

## Scenario

There were no messages on the floater and nothing on the hardsite intercept. So Bolan took a final climb up that pole as the first item of new business. First, he totally disabled the line to the hardsite, isolating them completely from the outside world. Then he initiated a call to Washington and waited impatiently as the clean line ran its tricky combinations.

Brognola came on with a huff. "Forget it, Striker. It's completely out of reach!"

"Give it to me."

"Somebody beat me to it. They hit the guy, right on the steps of the Senate office building!"

"It's okay," Bolan said.

"The hell it—what do you mean?"

"Get this very carefully, Hal. Every detail is important. It's a place called Club Taconic in the hills northwest of Pittsfield, on the old Hancock Turnpike. It's a hardsite now, with probably fifty guns defending it. It's also, I think, maybe the intended throne for the new empire. The guy is there right now, the guy behind it all, and I have the joint under siege. There's a hell of a good reason why I can't just level it and leave it."

"Angelina?"

"You got it. They're holding her in one of the bungalows. It's the one on the south end. Now

163

look, here's the lay. It's a big place with lots of open spaces inside the walls, plenty of vegetative cover outside. It's plenty hard. I doubt that I could get in there again, unless I really pull the cork on them. I guess that's what I'll have to do, because—"

"I'll take it over, Striker."

"I'd love it, Hal, but there isn't time. They're getting reinforcements at field battalion strength. Could be arriving at any moment. I'll have to just lay all over them and hope for the best. You try sending cops in there and that lady will be the first to die. You know it and I know it so let's not waste the time arguing. I'm going to spring her if I can. Meanwhile you'd better get a force moving this way. If I don't make it, then you'll have to play the lay any way you have left."

"I understand."

"Okay, there's more. I—just a minute."

"You okay?"

"Yeah, I . . ."

"You sound terrible. What is it?"

"Oh, there are a few hurts. I'm up a pole, Hal. Trying to get this damn belt away from raw flesh. Okay. I need to tell you about Sticker. He's on the way to Manhattan, right now. If he calls in, give him the straight. He has a right."

"Okay, sure. But isn't he headed the wrong way? There's still this problem with a dissolving cover."

"I think we have that shored up. At least we do have a play. Here's that scenario. You'll need to add a few props here and there. Someone has been angling for a tab on Leo. They dummied up a government house and killed a couple of feds, purely for effect. They have a boy in Washington who has already let it leak that a VIP informant is about to go public. The feds have been keeping

164

this VIP's family in that same government house. How does it read?"

"Sounds great, yeah."

"Okay, now someone is going to produce this informant's wife with the story that they took her from the safe house. Will that play to you?"

"If you're covering all the bases, sure. We can play to it beautifully."

"Okay. There's still an item missing, Hal. You need a patsy. To cover the real leak, I mean."

"I suppose you have one already in mind."

"Not yet. But I'll try to pick one up as I'm passing by. Cold meat, I think, would be best. Don't you?"

"That would make it much simpler, yes," Brognola agreed.

"Right. Okay. I'll try to leave you a package with the local cops. It will be neatly bundled and labeled."

"Let's see if I'm reading you, Striker. We do have this very real leak—not the imagined one. It's the one that got Angelina snatched—for real. Now you say that we're getting Angelina back and we're also covering Sticker with a scenario about a tab conspiracy. How'm I doing?"

"Right down the pike."

"Okay. A problem yet remains, then. We really do have that leak—a highly sensitive leak—and it's saying that some VIP *mafioso* is actually an undercover fed. Now. You're saying that we will provide a patsy to take that fall for Sticker, thus also relieving some heat in Washington town."

"That's it, yeah. We have to cover both fronts—yours and Leo's. I think that will cover it—and it should weaken the enemy while we're doing it. What it comes down to is this: you will have something to take into that Senate committee and say, okay, look fellows, here's the guy, he's dead as hell, I apologize for the irritation to your fine political sensitivities, but it's all over now, so let's forget it and be men. Then you schedule a hero's funeral and call a press conference or whatever you do in such messes—and hopefully the matter is ended. Does it play?"

"It plays, sure. Who're you going to send me?"

"I'll try for something not too small, not too large. But I'll have to take what I can get, if you're in a hurry-up situation."

Brognola sighed. "I'll take what I can get, Striker."

"Okay. I'll be trying, buddy."

"Glad to hear you calling me that. I was starting to wonder."

"I still love you, Hal. I just can't live with you."

The fed chuckled and said, "Go to hell. Okay. I suppose Sticker is up on the scenario."

"Most of it, yeah. I have to go, time's ticking."

"Right. Hey! God's sake, guy. I can't say be careful, can I? You wouldn't know what I meant."

Bolan chuckled grimly. "Careful doesn't win it, guy." He killed the patch, tidied up the pole, and went below to prepare the shootout.

And—no, Hal—there was no careful way for that.

# CHAPTER TWENTY-ONE

## Beside the Fire

Several things were still bothering Bolan as he made preparations for the showdown battle at Pittsfield.

He still did not understand why it was happening *here*. That troubling question remained: why Pittsfield? Why the territory that nobody wanted? He had thought that perhaps the answer lay in the hardsite itself. But he had seen nothing during the penetration to suggest that.

Why the big move on Leo Turrin? And why the fantastic lengths to track down the guy's family and snatch his wife from the safe house? After all was said and done, could it be that all this insanity was a direct result of Leo's undercover activities? Having found the guy out, would anyone go to such ridiculous lengths to take the guy out of the picture? That did not play, no. The action here was merely another stitch in the overall weave of intrigue which had lately been spreading throughout the Mafia world. For some reason, it had all become centered at Pittsfield. Why?

There were other troubling questions, entirely localized. Item: why was Simon's force huddled in fear in an old pleasure palace—one that had obviously been hastily and carelessly refurbished—directly under the muzzle of Bolan's "fantastic fire-

167

works"—simply sitting and awaiting the intervention of a rescue force? Why had they not simply come out on their own to face the challenge? No, it did not play.

Even more puzzling, why had they continued to sit and wait even while Bolan was scrambling for his own life after an aborted penetration? Why had they not seized that opportunity to break clear, to find a "more defensible" position? And, yeah, it all kept coming back to the idea of *defense*, didn't it? What the hell were they defending?

Granted—Simon was no dummy. But look at his actions. Or, rather, his reactions. With Bolan's first shot at the site, the guy went into a stonewall defense. He pulled everybody inside and sent for help. Was that rational? If Bolan could blow a car off the driveway with a single blow, then he sure as hell could blow the house out from under them.

Except, remember, Simon was no dummy. He would think like an Ace. Bolan shot a car with two "boys" in it. He did not shoot a house with fifty boys and a commissioner in it. Ergo, Bolan could not shoot the house.

Okay. So the guy went out and tried to make the logic fit. He looked up into those hills and asked, "Where is he?" And he drew a line and made a fix on a gun emplacement which could target on the front gate and drive but not on the house. And since the house had not yet been attacked, the probability was very good that the "gun" could not be properly emplaced for an attack on the house.

And what about that dramatic, wild-ass attempt to physically penetrate the joint? Okay. There would be a logic to explain that one, also. Bolan was not operating alone on this one. He had help. Obviously the guy could not have shot his own car

168

from under himself using a gun emplaced in the hills far away. Maybe that would explain why Simon sat and awaited rescue instead of breaking while Bolan was scrambling. The same guy who had shot Bolan's car away could shoot theirs away, as well.

So, okay. A logic was there. But Bolan was still not satisfied with it.

He was still bothered, sure, but that did not alter his opinions. There were no options to be altered. He had to go down there and snatch that lady back. Period, end of options.

To accomplish that, he would need everything within reach going for him. Everything within reach was contained in the technological triumph which Bolan called "the warwagon." Plus, of course, the man himself. So it was going to require a team effort. The machine and the man—that was the team.

Would that be enough?

The whole answer lay in the versatility of the fire system. The "intrusion" type of automatic fire had already proven effective as a siege weapon. A different capability would be required for any sort of realistic infantry support. Such a system, modeled to the man's unique situation, had been provided. It was called "EVA Control"—"EVA" meaning extra-vehicular activity. Under this mode, the man operated outside the vehicle for a one-mile-range limit and "commanded" the fire via a radio-remote control blackbox which was about the size of a pack of king cigarettes.

It worked in the following way: Prior to commencement of "EVA," target acquisition was preprogrammed for as many as four specific stationary targets. The system was then cycled to "EVA Control," which immediately placed the fire system on "Fire Enable Standby." The remote blackbox had four buttons, one for each pre-selected target track. The man merely depressed the button for the target desired ... and a bird would fly. A firebird, yeah.

That was the way Bolan set it up for the showdown battle at Pittsfield. That is, for the machine side of the team. For the man himself, there were the standard, less exotic weapons of war. An M-16/M-79 combo—with plenty of ammo for both the lightning-fast, fully automatic machine gun, as well as for the big-punch cannon with her high-explosive, smoke, buck, or gas capability.

Also, for the man, there was the standby .44 Auto-Mag sidearm in military web to ride the right thigh, plus enough clips of brainbusters to keep the big piece thundering through a sustained firefight.

And then there were the miscellaneous personal munitions which dangled from shoulder and chest straps, within easy reach of a needy hand.

Taken all together, it seemed a formidable enough team. But that was an illusion of technology. Actually, the team was the man, and the man was the team. All of it hinged upon his ability to move through the fire and to take that fire to the other side.

Bolan had no illusions in that respect. It all came down finally, wholly, every time, to the man himself.

So far, the man had always been equal to the task. This time, he was not so positive about that. But he was as ready as he would ever be. And time was short.

So it was time to take the fire to the enemy.

It was time, yeah, to see who was the greatest savage of all.

He left the machine in firing alignment a hundred yards out and closed on foot, straight down the pike along the trail of broken cars.

There was no way they could not have seen him coming. Apparently they were waiting him in, taking his stride and intent—wondering, maybe, what the hell the guy thought he was up to this time, just walking in like that in broad daylight, and in full combat regalia.

And maybe some of them were remembering that daring sprint along this same path such a short while earlier—and waiting for it again.

· The man stepped past the clutter at the gate, aware that he was approaching the end of wonderment. As he stepped onto that turf, he summoned the machine. A firebird leapt to the response, whistling in along the right flank with a rush of rustling air to presage the loosing of the thunderclap.

The fiery spirit of romance staggered that old building and sent sections of it lofting skyward upon turrets of fire, taking wonder with it and spreading panic and despair where wonder had been.

The man walked on, following the circle of pavement as electrified savages poured forth upon the shores of the fire, bawling and stampeding in doomsday bedlam. He sent them more, via the bellowing M-79, as he continued the encirclement and closed surely on the paydirt he sought in the last bungalow south.

The machine sent another, this one spreading the illumination of technology across savage pastures, turning the bawling herd from the south lawn and

171

forcing them into the contest of man against men. Shotguns boomed and choppers rattled as some deeper pride goaded the response to challenge. The M-16 sang back its lightning lullaby of the grave, knowing no empty songs or wasted lyrics.

And the man walked on, in search of a female who had on place in this realm of madness but deserved a more joyous place—one where the basic orientation was toward life and not toward death—to the civil, not the savage.

Another frantic volley demanded his attention, diverting his steps momentarily as three gasping romantics dropped from an upper window with clothing aflame. They had seen the fire and lingered too long in wonder. He sent them peace and wishes for a better trip the next time around, then went on to his goal.

He knew that he was bleeding at the neck—though he felt no pain there—and his left arm had suddenly grown intensely heavy. Four wild-eyed candidates for soulhood lunged across his path and promptly regretted the indiscretion as a floral wreath of dancing tumblers descended upon them and broke them open and lay them down, all as one.

And now he had the taste of blood upon his lips and felt a warmth across his chest.

He summoned the fire again and brought it convulsing into that staggering old structure behind him. It was too much on top of too much; the fire spilled over and bounced onto those other roofs, even to the last one south.

Flames were leaping all along that line of travel when he reached the goal and kicked the door away. He dropped the weapon and snatched back a swooning little Italian housewife, and he went out again through the flames.

The naked form was draped across the deadening shoulder and the thundering AutoMag was in the good hand, clearing the withdrawal path as savages caught the smell of blood and rushed to fill the pot with the largest savage of all.

But the largest savage was not yet down nor yet alone. He did not fear the fire.

*Three away!*

*Four away!*

The fire swept in and the man walked out with his burden—not a cross, but a gentle person who deserved a gentle world.

He took the woman to the machine, the gentlest world he had, then returned to the fire.

He found none who had passed the test—but one struggled on beside the inferno.

The guy looked as though he had climbed inside the fire to examine it from within. He was blackened and split, yet somehow alive and aware, writhing in his own bitter juices and moaning for help from a God he had spurned too long ago.

Bolan's eyes twitched at the pitiful sight of that as he raised the AutoMag to end it mercifully. But then the guy spoke to him. The voice was beyond recognition, but those curiously stilted words were unmistakably familiar.

"Give it to me, Bolan! Don't make me beg for it!"

With that recognition, some stubborn savage anger refused to die in the man. The voice was cold and the fury evident as he replied, "You've been begging for it all your life, Simon. You tell me why you begged for it in Pittsfield and I'll give it to you, guy."

Those tortured eyes traveled up through the

173

flames to where he'd been when the fire came down. A flame-wrapped bed hung out there, half spilled over through the shattered wall of that "one big suite" of the upper story. It was a strangely shaped contraption, burdened with medical gadgets, overlarge and massive, with handcranks at each end. The charred mattress still partially supported an even more charred human body—or, at least, half a body.

And suddenly there were no questions left in Mack Bolan.

He put a bullet between the pleading eyes beside the fire, dropped a marksman's medal upon that romantic breast, and went away from there.

No more questions, no.

Bolan realized that he had found "Jesus"—if those biblical code names really had significance.

"The man" was the last of a line, the King of Kings, Little Augie Marinello.

And he'd died in the territory nobody wanted.

# EPILOGUE

Angelina was still having trouble meeting the Bolan gaze. The problem, he knew, had nothing to do with the bullet she'd put in him long ago, during that first time around the track at Pittsfield. No—it was something closer and much more intimate to a woman. She was a hell of a pretty one, and there was no reason for the continued embarrassment; there was nothing there to hide and certainly not to be ashamed of. It wasn't her fault they'd stripped her naked and thrown her in a bare cage.

She poured the coffee and bent down to plant a quick kiss on Leo's nose, then excused herself and returned to the kitchen area.

"You're a hell of a lucky man, Leo," Bolan murmured.

"Call it charmed," the new commissioner replied, grinning. "As for you, soldier, I think you must have a guardian angel." He reached across the table to tenderly lift the corner of a gauze pad at the side of Bolan's neck. "That looks mad as hell. Another silly centimeter, buddy, and neither of you would've gotten out of there. How's the shoulder?"

"It will mend," Bolan assured him. How about yours? Are you sure it's firmed up with Eritrea?"

"It's firmed, yeah. I'm better than ever. I don't

even need that guy, now. Hell of a card player he turned into. He gave me away to the *Commissione*."

Bolan smiled sourly. "That's fine. Because I've about decided to give him away."

"What does that mean?"

"I promised Hal a patsy. Cold meat. I didn't have anything left to deliver it with, though. I think I'll give him some warm meat."

Leo's eyes widened. "David?"

Bolan nodded soberly. "The one and only. The guy earned it. Look, Leo—Simon was ten times the man this guy is. At least he died with his chief. Stood by the old man's dying cause to the bitter end."

"I still don't know how that got engineered," Leo said. "Did you say that—did David really mean to . . ."

"I don't know it for certain, Leo. Maybe we never will. It's a crazy bunch. How do you figure a logic with crazy people? The fact remains that David Eritrea had been sitting in Augie Marinello's chair since Jersey. Augie has been sitting up here on your doorstep for the past two weeks. So David has been desperately buying time and riding his horse clear to the gates of hell. Billy Gino thought the old man was still in Long Island, all this time."

"Yeah, that's what he said. And he still doesn't know how to take this with David."

"A lot of people won't." Bolan sighed heavily. "I'll tell you what I believe, Leo. I believe Augie was fighting desperately just to remain alive. David had taken over just about the whole damn thing. Augie got wind of it, and somehow he managed to get himself out of there. Probably via Simon and the other Aces he could rally to the cause. But

Augie has been dying in pieces for a long time. Absolutely bedridden and probably kept alive by all sorts of heroic means. They must have known it was all hopeless—so why did they do it? Romance, that's why. They needed to put him some place cool. What better place than Pittsfield? Close enough to Manhattan—yet, really, very isolated from the mob's traffic patterns. It was the territory nobody wanted. The Aces figured to nudge you out of the picture to completely safe the territory. And they joined together in this last cling to the king routine, started running around the country collecting old debts, brokering for enough power to at least scare hell out of David Eritrea and back the guy down long enough for Augie to die with a bit of dignity. That's all they could have hoped for. I had the thing reversed. And I guess I played right into David's hand of cards. I put down the final operation and you sealed it with a kiss. David is now home clean."

Leo sighed. "Well, I know it's a crazy world, Sarge. But I really thought that old man liked me more than that. I mean, he could have taken me into it—or at least tried. He didn't have to contract me, then run out and snatch my woman."

Bolan gave him a piercing look and said, "Be realistic, guy."

Turrin chuckled soberly. "You're right."

"The hell of it is, buddy, they had you snockered. All of a sudden it didn't really matter whether you lived or died. As long as they had Angelina in the pocket—and considering where they took her from—well, you were a dead man any way they looked at it."

Leo shivered slightly. His gaze rose beyond Bo-

177

lan to the busy figure of his "little Italian house-wife."

"She wants to go get the kids, Sarge. She won't sit down until we do."

Bolan smiled as he gazed at the woman. "Well, if that's where the joy is . . ."

"That's where it is, sure."

Bolan said. "Okay. You people get the hell out of here. Do me a favor, though. First chance, get a message off to Al Weatherbee. Let him know how this thing all wrapped out. Alice worries."

Leo chuckled. "So do I. Where does the war take you next, buddy?"

"You want to go along?"

"Hell no." The little guy stood up and rapped his knuckles against the warwagon's false wall. "Knock on wood. You have my new number. I can really feed you now, guy. Keep you so damn busy you won't have time to run around saving dumb asses like mine."

The Bolan gaze was soberly warm as he replied to that. "It's the worthiest save I ever made, Leo. Believe it. Now take your lady out of here. I need to call Hal and discuss a scenario for a warm patsy."

"How will you engineer that?"

"That's a whole 'nother story, Leo."

Angelina came back, stared at him soberly for a moment, then bent down and hung a moist kiss squarely on the startled Bolan lips.

"I love your home," she whispered. "It's very nice."

Bolan stood at the door and watched until long after the man and his woman had faded completely into the New York night.

"The first fire," he soberly told himself, "was built by a woman."

Yeah. And it would take the guys the balance of eternity to put the damn thing out.

He looked around him, at the awesome technologies nestled there, and thought of Angelina's parting words.

It was nice, yeah. And it was not a grave; it was a way of life.

More, even, this *was* Mack Bolan's home. It was where the heart was.